D1195178

Other titles by this author

The Iguana

A Music Behind the Wall, Volume One

Anna Maria Ortese

A Music Behind the Wall

Selected Stories

VOLUME TWO

Translated from the Italian

by Henry Martin

McPherson & Company

For information, address the publisher: McPherson & Company, Post Office Box 1126, Kingston, New York 12402. Production of this book has been assisted by a publication grant from the literature program of the New York State Council on the Arts and a translation grant from the National Endowment for the Arts, a federal agency. Designed by Bruce McPherson. Typeset in Bodoni Book. The paper is neutral pH for permanence. Manufactured in the United States of America.

1 3 5 7 9 10 8 6 4 2 1998 1999 2000 2001
FIRST EDITION

Library of Congress Cataloging-in-Publication Data

Ortese, Anna Maria.
[Short Stories. English. Selections.]
A music behind the wall : selected stories / Anna Maria Ortese ; translated by Henry Martin
v. < 2 > ; cm.
ISBN 0-929701-56-9 (cloth) : $22.00
1. Ortese, Anna Maria—Translations into English. 1. Martin, Henry, 1942- . II. Title.
PQ4875.R8A25 1998
853'.914—dc20 94-7229

Four of these translations first appeared in the magazines *Conjunctions*, *Alea*, *Third Coast*, *Cups* and *www.Archipelago.org*. The original Italian stories were first published as follows: "Redskin" as "Pellerossa" in the collection *Angelici dolori*, Bompianim Milan, 1937 and 1942; and slightly revised and bearing the title "Piel Roja e il fanciullo Apasa (Comanche)," as a section of the novel *Il Porto di Toledo*, Rizzoli, Milan, 1975 and 1985. "The Villa" as "La villa" in the collection *Angelici dolori*. "Slanting Eyes" as "Occhi obliqui," and "The Great Street" as "Grande via" in the collection *L'infanta sepolta*, Sera Editrice, Milan, 1950. "A Night at the Station" as "Una notte nella stazione" in the collection *Silenzio a Milano*, Bari, 1958. "Fantasies" as "Fantasticherie," and "The Gray Halo" as "L'alone grigio," in the collection *L'alone grigio*, Valecchi editore, Florence, 1969. "Nebel (A Lost Story)" as "Nebel (racconto perduto)," and "Folletto in Genoa" as "La morte del Folletto," in the collection *In sonno e in veglia*, Adelphi, Milan, 1987. "Where Time Is Another" as "Dove il tempo è un altro" in *Micromega 5/90*, Rome, 1990.

CONTENTS

FOREWORD

This second volume of English translations of Anna Maria Ortese's stories finds its points of departure, like the first, in the seven collections of shorter fictions which the author published between 1937, the date of the first edition of *Angelici dolori*, and 1987, when *In sonno e in veglia* appeared; and it also presents an extended self-portrait—"Where Time Is Another"—that was published in 1990 (though written in 1980) in *Micromega* magazine.

Fictions, personal recollections, travel reports, philosophical reflections, and journalistic reportage don't stand at all apart from one another in Anna Maria Ortese's work. The narrative "I" which she develops in her novels and stories seems often to court its own possible resemblance to an autobiographical "I"—the narrative voice is almost always a woman's voice, and often the voice of a woman writer of an age not very different from the age Ortese herself would have been at the time of the writing of the story—or to function perhaps as a kind of experimentation of a view which the author might possibly hold, or long to hold, or hope to exorcise, of herself; and, on the other hand, her explicitly autobiographical writings take on their brightest life and most crystalline meaning at the moment of a *denouement* or sudden self-reassessment, thus turning themselves into lessons or epiphanies, much as happens in fiction. Identity is one of the mysteries that Anna Maria Ortese most subtly and constantly explores, one of the conundrums she attempts most stubbornly to crack, and she seems to suggest that identity is always uncertain, perilous and hypothetical, or always, at best, in the making. So it makes little difference if the "I" with which she deals is real or fictional, since the problem is in any case to cleanse both perception and imagination, provoking their realignment, and allowing each to rediscover the curative powers of the other.

Anna Maria Ortese's work is never about facts or events, whether real or imagined, but always about relationships to facts and events, or about drawing facts and events into a context that lets them make sense. Her one fundamental perception, as she tells us in "Where Time Is Another," is that "the world *is a heavenly body*, that all things within and beyond the world are made of cosmic matter; and that their nature, their meaning—except for a dazzling gentleness—is unsoundable." This, she tells us, is something that children understand, and which adults have ceased to understand. Similar words appear in "The Submerged Continent," in Volume One of this collection: "...every child should be informed right from the start that the Earth is a ball *suspended* in space, a modest pebble lost within a universe which in turn is lost among other universes; then they need to be advised that it is *very unlikely*, no matter how potent the tools possessed by the last man on earth, that we will ever know the nature of these other universes." She sees her highest experience of the world, again in "Where Time Is Another," as the experience of its "strangeness," and her voices and characters achieve their identity in the moment in which they are able to do this strangeness justice—this strangeness and its dazzling gentleness.

Ortese's voices and protagonists are always somehow astray, and often in the midst of a search of which they are less than fully aware. Some fail, others succeed. There is never, moreover, any "key" to success, nor any tacit error leading inevitably to ruin. Grace remains inexplicable. The world through which these voices and protagonists move is always more complex than they can hope to be, yet the maze of their own sensibilities is one of the places in which that world is able to conceal and reveal its surprises. So, the guide to which Ortese's characters turn while making their way through themselves is, at best, a sense of uneasiness, openly and thoroughly accepted, which serves as a kind of compass that leads from riddle to riddle and from one sore point to the next, and finally, perhaps, to a moment of greater understanding. Horizons widen unexpectedly, as though in response to a special form of courage. Tenacity and honesty, in the world Ortese shows us, are much more important than intelligence, or count perhaps as essential components of a special form of intelligence, partly archaic and partly new. One of Ortese's heroines remarks—in "Winter Voyage," which appears in Volume One—"Who knows if I'll be able to say exactly what I think? (But perhaps *exactly* is not at all *the way* I think, and there you have it.)"

Folletto in Genoa

The gravity of political events is at times unendurable. And the use of the word "political" is a euphemism. We live in the midst of a war, or a malady, and we watch the advance of a tireless, bludgeoning violence which slithers like tongues of fire over the whole of the earth. At moments the various conflagrations threaten to conjoin. A billow of smoke—of news, confusion and calamity—seems all-pervasive, and is everywhere at large. The sky, even at its bluest, appears to veer towards lead. A bitter heaviness, as though of drunkenness, or as though our lives were about to end (and had proved entirely useless), weighs like a mountain on the human heart.

I found myself in just this state of mind a few years back, owing, I believe, to a fresh act of villainy which was about to be consummated between two lands I will not name, to the detriment of a third and wholly impoverished, not to say "wretched" country, it moreover being clear that these first two nations, in turn, had been spurred and I might say blinded—if such blindness, even more than deliberate, were not self-interested—by two other nations, both of which were far too intelligent to confront one another directly, and I'll hope to be forgiven for circumlocution. Life on the earth, at this particular moment, struck me not, I'll say, as unbearable (that stage already had been surpassed) but as utterly despoiled of even the slightest interest, like a stone roiling forward from out of eternity and off toward another eternity of stone. My dismay, on this one morning, was in fact so taut that, having made the trip to Genoa to dispense with a piece of highly tedious business (at the District Office of Public Properties), I had forgotten to make my return to the railway station, as surely would have been logical. Especially since it was snowing, in spite, or so I seem to recall, of its being the month of May. In short, I first had gone to the port, where I saw nothing but black on white; and then to the hills, where it was all exactly the same, except in reverse; and finally I had wandered to a dark and squalid quarter of town where I had never been before, it appeared. So by then it must have been close to four in the afternoon—and the season was beginning to reassert its mettle—when I found myself in the act of climbing a run-down stone ramp, hidden behind a tree, and then a flight of stairs, narrower and steeper (perhaps of slate), which was reached by way of a low and decrepit courtyard door; and here still again with no idea of where I might be going. I was tired of this world, quite simply.

On reaching the sixth floor, I encountered the happy surprise of an open door, the last, and of hearing familiar voices, two of them, in the room beyond it: the voices of a man and a woman, in a somewhat rising tone, which I recognized as belonging to Eulalio Ramo and his sister Ruperta Ramo, a seamstress. Ruperta had once been married, long before, to another Ramo (a distant cousin) and that was her only reason for allowing herself to be called by a name which she shared with a brother whom she detested: one of those piercing, venomous and implacable hatreds that sometimes arise between unhappy relatives or other people who share a roof. Ruperta was crazy, by nature and owing as well to that ill-conceived marriage, whereas Eulalio—generally addressed as *Signor Lalio*—was a half-wit. What bound them together, aside from her hatred and his timidity, was their mutual solitude, and also his pension, as a civil invalid, which when added to her earnings allowed them both to get by without excessive hardship even in times, like these, which are clearly problematic. They were both about fifty (which at least is how I remembered them from the previous time I had seen them; and that, it seemed, was the state in which I rediscovered them) but both of them looked much older. She, with her squarish face and smallish bones, was short and stout, and must once, now gray, have been brunette. He was tall and lanky, and when younger must have been blond, as indeed he had remained. But blond like a corpse, which is to say with a strangely withered face, half asleep and absent.

I had met them—I had been in that house, as I then recalled, some ten, or was it fifteen years before—at the time when their tragedy was beginning; and now, automatically, I had returned. So that explained the mystery.

But only up to a certain point: the nature of their squabble was quite disconcerting—its subject was a certain Folletto, a "Pixie," whom Ruperta now wanted to ban from her room, saying she was simply "fed up," and since when might pixies have lived in that house?—and a wall I seemed to remember as having stood directly in front of the entrance, a red wall, was no longer there. In its place I confronted a short uncarpeted flight of stairs, lit by a very dim bulb. Ruperta stood at the top of those stairs, with an enormous pair of shears in her hand—which was comprehensible, given her profession as a seamstress—and she thrust them about as she shouted:

"I've no more pity to spare! Starting right now, *Stellino mio*, my little star," her tone derisive, "is nobody's business but yours, you understand me? You're to keep him to yourself, downstairs, and he might as well forget about these steps."

"But please, Rupina, you know I'd never ask you to help take care of him, I can manage that alone," Lalio, who to me was out of sight, retorted, "but he'll die without you. Stellino has lived in your room for a hundred and ten years. He was the apple of your eye, and now he can't do without you… Come on, let him back in."

The woman made no reply, but violently yanked into place a curtain of shabby damask, in which I promptly recognized the missing "wall." Meanwhile, however, she had seen me—but unfortunately without recognizing me, or perhaps without seeing any reason to admit to having done so. She quickly grew quite proper, nodding acknowledgment of my presence, and inquired hypocritically *how she might be of help to me…*

At precisely that moment, an utterly curious creature dressed in a brief cape made of old newspapers—these papers aglare with all the more and less alarming reports which had driven my melancholy to a pitch and thereby directed my path to that house—and this cape still further embellished with numerous strips of tattered red plush, which clearly were scraps left over from tailoring—advanced with a halting gait from a part of the room which till then had remained out of sight to me; and on reaching the flight of stairs, he began a laborious climb towards the object of his whole devotion; but the woman had taken off a shoe and hurtled it down at him. Though he had not been hit, Stellino, the aforementioned, stopped in his tracks as though chagrined.

He was a creature I will not attempt to describe. It

wouldn't be civil to say I know I wouldn't be believed, but surely the tale would arouse all sorts of perplexities. Perplexities, I have to admit, that baffled me as well. He was no taller…than a child just a few years old, and even, in fact, much smaller than that—the size of a doll—and with a body—especially the legs, which peeped from beneath the newspaper print—that resembled the figure of a russet—or grayish?—hare. An abundance of golden-grayish fur, but white around the chin. On his head, a polka-dot kerchief, knotted at the top. His skull was round, beneath that ludicrous scrap of cloth, and his long black ears were pointed. And if ever eyes had attempted to thieve the splendor of crystal, and the sweet sadness of the opal and the amethyst, those were Stellino's eyes. He looked at the woman as though to say, "Ruperta, dearest mother Ruperta, why can't I stay in your room any longer, why can't I have your company? I feel so awful…so truly awful. Your little Stellino will die from it. Please, dearest Ruperta, mother Ruperta, let me stay with you."

"It's that tooth! I've already told you, and I'm telling you again! So take him to the dentist," Ruperta newly screamed, after a moment in which, to me—judging from what struck me as an unnatural silence—she had seemed to be battling with her own emotions. Then, turning in my direction, she repeated, curtly, "Can I help you?"

The telephone rang upstairs in her room and thus disposed of the question, likewise reprieving me from quite an outlandish reply: ("I had come to pick up *my dress!*") A client, perhaps a tourist, calling from one of Genoa's snowy hilltops, was on the phone, as was instantly clear from the flattering, servile tone assumed by Lalio's sister. She bustled, "…but I'm on my way! *Certainement…* I'll be there in a half hour *ma chère, …*" but with a mixture of disdain and sickening affectation that deformed the fine

French phrase, concluding, "*...j'en suis très satisfaite, Madame...*"

Five minutes to dress in a tailored suit that might best have befitted an old gendarme—a suit, moreover, less graced than blasted by a silk tricolor cravat (the Italian flag, though without the coat of arms). And then having grasped a sizable crocodile bag, its open maw unclasped, along with a stocky umbrella which resembled a billy-club, she precipitated down the stairs. Or, better, she appeared to precipitate, given her bulk, though in fact she descended them staidly, and with not so much as a glance at her miserable admirer. She simply insisted, "Out of here! Get him out of here, Lalio, and I mean it; and when he has to make dirt, take him into your room..." Lalio, as she passed, gathered the poor sick creature into his arms.

Folletto's little pixie face—but "Folletto" is the only description which truly suits him, and moreover the only name by which his species was known in that house—rested in the crook of the poor old half-wit's arm. And his amethyst eyes (with those glints of crystal) turned now toward Lalio's sad and wrinkled face, now toward the door through which, just earlier, I had entered and through which Ruperta meanwhile had left. Never before—I can say so quite truthfully—had I seen the eyes of a Christian (or even a pagan) to show such love and supplication for a woman, and all for so horrid a species of woman as this Ruperta; nor had I ever seen so great an indifference to the delicate, frightening love of a pixie, to his ceaseless torment and gentle entreaties, as in the eyes of this terrible seamstress.

Once the woman was gone, Folletto, whom Lalio had set back down on the floor, immediately made his dirt, as though until then having retained it out of fear and horror at the thought of a blow that *she* might have dealt him. He made his dirt under the table, vomiting as well, and then lay sulking beneath a dilapidated wardrobe full of dresses ready to be delivered—as you could tell from the identical plastic covers that protected the shoulders of the garments, and also because the wardrobe had no doors. Lalio, before thinking to deal with the mess, bent down to this poor fantastic creature to speak soothingly to him; and I was happy, knowing my way about the house, to take care of the cleaning up myself. I also opened the door onto the balcony—which at one end surmounted a gully, and at the other end an ancient snow-laden alleyway—to let in a bit of fresh air, which meanwhile had begun to stir.

The world, in that brief space of time, seemed to have changed. It seemed to have grown meeker, and was almost charged with laughter (even in spite of ubiquitous desperation). You no longer remembered, or no longer focused on the day's dark menaces... As though all its oppressions, and all its preposterous sequels of jeers and threats (the marks of hostilities that also, as I myself had seen, scourged the goodness of Nature while strewing their fateful anguish through the miserable lives of human beings) contained a touch of playfulness... As though this World were only joking... An enormous cloud, there toward the west, gray in a cold yellow sky, now seemed Ruperta herself, the woman of hate, receding into the distance with her enormous seamstress' shears.

From Lalio's lips, as at first he knelt and then as he sat on a low chair beside Folletto—who meanwhile seemed to have fallen asleep, or who might have appeared to be stunned by drugs (his amethyst eyes remaining fixed, through the open balcony door, on a cloud)—I learned the whole of the tragedy of their recent years. And here I abandoned *remembering*, since nothing at all of that part of their lives was known to me. It went back further than our uncertain acquaintance. Ruperta, according to Lalio, had once, in Canicattì, the town where they were born, been a lively and very beautiful girl—an utterly regal beauty with whom the fascinating Don Vito Cologero, from Catania, had fallen in love. Finally she had married him. And on moving to her new home in the northern city of Genoa, where her Sicilian husband had emigrated, she had taken along not only her idiot brother, but the delicate Folletto as well. An era of miracles, of a grace that Saint Rosalia herself... She would sing all day long... But Folletto harbored objections, since he loved his Ruperta with a love that declared her unshareable. So Stellino, during the night, had set to "praying." Sadly enough, and there was proof. (As the idiot talked, Folletto had opened his eyes and seemed to entreat, "Enough, my master, enough! Take pity, and spare me!") He prayed "to his people." And soon those prayers were heard. Don Vito met up with another woman, and her name was Constance, which is a name that holds no promise of anything good. For a while he kept up appearances, but finally he confessed: he had promised himself to Constance for life: "You, Ruperta dear, are older than I am, and you have to understand..." The scenes that followed, naturally enough, were fit to send souls to damnation...but things like that can be found in any novel. In any case, Ruperta found succor in her sense of pride, and one fine day, on her own initiative, she told the man she loved that he had to go... "Not, you see, that he *could* go, but that he *had* to go, which is different... It was really splendid. Folletto," as the idiot further recounted, "couldn't believe his prayers had been answered, but," Lalio continued, "he had badly sized things up with Ruperta. Along with her womanly happiness, Ruperta had also banished, and forever, her girlishness (since a girl was what, until then, she had always remained inside of herself.) To make a long story short, she began to despise her brother, and then, even worse, the poor Folletto, who," the idiot explained, "had always lived in the Ramo family home, at first with the brothers and sister, and *even earlier* with their parents, and their grandparents, and finally back to their great grandparents and that brigand by the name of Giacinto *Ramo* Marino—from before the era of Garibaldi—who had 'found' him on the hearth at the time when he bought the house..." "Found him?" I interrupted, fairly befuddled. "Yes, he found him, the mischievous little thing, in front of the fire where he was saying his little 'prayers'...to the dead, to the genies, to the spirits of the past...all, he said, for the family's prosperity, but equally"—this, I understood, was Lalio's suspicion—"to assure the success of his childish pranks on the cats and the finches, to make no mention of assuring the failure of Garibaldi (though later he changed his mind!)"

Yes, because Folletto was a *child*; he had been born a child, and now was dying as a child: an entirely illogical and innocent creature, even in spite, as I had just then heard, of his hundred and twelve years of age... The unification of Italy.

As I listened to the words of this poor demented man—yet hardly more demented and much more gentle than his flaming sister—I subsided into something like drowsiness, a spell that barred me from grasping reality. I could see that this curious fool was dreaming, or taking his revenge on someone; I could see that Ruperta was quite unhappy, and that all her unhappiness resided first of all in her "firmness" (not to say her rigidity); and I could see that Stellino—*Stellino mio*—suffered atrociously. Of that there could be no doubt. Though perhaps there was room for doubt as to what he truly was. Gnome, fairy, elf, an angel from the skies? I was nearly afraid to cast a further glance at the space between two chairs where his bed of shredded paper lay. Apparently a beast, a cat, but perhaps an October hare, or a lunar squirrel. But his face—whether of cat, hare or lunar squirrel—wore so sublime an expression of the unloved and loving child: in the snout that grew ever more pointed, and in the splendid amethyst eyes, at their corners two barely perceptible stars which dawned and fled, like memories, like angels of the past. "Ah, little mother, my Ruperta," the unhappy Folletto would murmur now and then (surely I was dreaming) while from his mouth (the lips and palate of purest ebony) a strand of tenuous golden bubbles trailed down onto the noble little creature's matted breast... Words, perhaps unformulated thoughts, but not for that reason less real...

(As I write, I vaguely catch the sound of the wind blowing along the stairs: I am still in the sleepy province of Genoa, and a January night is about to fall. I return, absorbed, to telling my tale.)

That tiny emaciated body, forsaken beneath a cape snipped from old newsprint (where one still made out the headlines of a previous world war), and with a kerchief on its head—that kerchief which spoke of the gentleness of human affections, and from which, as well, there sprouted two black, attentive ears—everything about him was laughable...there was nothing one might take seriously...if not for the puny careworn hand that rested over his heart, a hand more similar to a sprig of rosemary than to a true human paw (thus my thoughts babbled on), what with its little fingernails all twisted sideways, by now disregarded, no longer groomed, and misshapen. Yes, I could understand that by now he had reached the mark of ONE HUNDRED AND TWELVE YEARS! (as the two mad siblings referred to presumably twelve or eighteen) and that creatures such as these are generally prone at such an age to take their leave, to vanish, and to die! But those wonderful violet eyes, brimming with tears, and continuing still to search about the ceiling or the skies for the monumental woman with whom he had shared his era of happiness...those eyes were those of a being *born a child*: as a member of the race of children: and that as such would die. He would die as the immortal *Pixie*—the immortal Folletto—which he was. And only the illness (more psychological than anything else) and the dogged, lunatic suffering, debasement, and often blind reactions of his two pain-ridden masters had made him a creature of Evil—a frightened little creature devoted to naughty pranks. But *Stellino*—the little star—was far from Evil incarnate (and not simply, perhaps, the incarnation of Good): he was the Spirit of Life which once so gladdened our fine and happy families, transfiguring this silly Boot into a mystic Garden! That alone is what he was; and now, along with him, all of it was coming to an end; and rose-blushed Dawn, no matter if every rampart might be battered down, was no longer thinkable!

Lalio, his face now streaked with tears (clearly, even his imbecility was less than total), had taken out a handkerchief edged in black—a mourner's handkerchief—but with a decorative pattern of tiny colorful pennants; and while kneeling at the flank of the dying sprite, he dried the creature's eyes... Folletto twitched an ear. He had heard footsteps on the stairs...but they had not come from *her!*

The half-wit told me (with great decorum, though ever more meekly dropping his head and revealing his withered neck), he told me, or re-evoked, the whole of the enormous tragedy which that ill-considered marriage had brought down upon the house, and which then had lapsed into reprisal against that cunning little creature (who in fact was a *non*-traditional spirit, just as I had supposed—simply vital, impassioned, and full of dreams) and of how in that place, that house, there had ceased to be further room for him. He described all the pains of the pixie's *ruination*, from the time when Ruperta had no longer wanted to keep him in her room, to the slow and ferocious derangement of her soul after Don Vito had set up house with Constance (and Ruperta's youth was forever finished). How she then had begun to torment and mortify Folletto! Perhaps, also, as a way of directing her rage at him, at Lalio: to prove to him that she was *free*, now, of feelings; that she had become a new woman...(such strange vengeance). Upstairs, in Ruperta's room, Stellino was no longer welcome. Whenever she walked through the house on her way to the kitchen, always wielding her enormous shears, his effusions were condemned to absolute blindness, or were rewarded with a kick. Yet Stellino refused to give in: he was always on the wait for her, like a panhandler. "And now," came Lalio's concluding remark, shaping a lie with incredible calm and fellow-feeling, "now we surely didn't need to see things worsened by this infected tooth... He's got an infected tooth; that's what he's dying from... But only, of course...*only if he doesn't take his medicine.*"

He then stood up to fetch a bowl of water and a teaspoonful of a pinkish powder which he raised to Stellino's black lips.

The pixie emitted a groan, moved only slightly, and the powder and the water spilled across his breast, which was already matted with vomit and tears.

I don't know why it came to mind, given such *distances*, by now insuperable, of nature and time, but I remembered an old southern song that spoke of childhood love, and it reminded me in turn of another: the sublime *Ballad* of Bernart de Ventadorn:

> As I see the jocund skylark
> rise, upleaping toward the sun,
> and then descend forgetfully
> to a sweeting who his heart hath won,
> so great an envy fills me
> for those whose joy I see,
> that for my heart not then to faint
> with longing, would surely count as wonder...

Which surely had nothing at all to do with Stellino's "martyrdom"... Yet he too was dying for a skylark: for the delicate love which bound him to the woman who once had been his mother, the immense and brute reality that strides with its shears across the sky, slicing everything into tatters, trampling and humiliating...

So how—or in what—might she inspire such fatal love?

> Ah, I thought I knew so much
> of love, yet know so little.

Half an hour later, having taken, as God commanded, a bit of that potion for his tooth (allowing that love and a toothache can be much the same), the poor Folletto was asleep, or so Lalio assured me, since by now the little breast was motionless, whereas his great, gentle (and vaguely cross-eyed) eyes were open and fixed: a strange hypnotic dormancy—or something more than that. "Yes, he's asleep," I said to myself, "asleep and dreaming of Paradise, dreaming of his own dear Ruperta, of her youth, when both of them were children, there in their land of flowers—not the frightful Sicily of today, nor this Liguria all thorns and desert—he's dreaming of the ancient land of flowers of which he was the gentle genie, the grace..."

Farewell, child; farewell Folletto!

It was time for me to go; night was approaching, and everything was extremely peaceful, just as when Lalio too and I myself had been children, and nothing like this leaden sky existed; it had always and only been blue, and there were boughs of almonds everywhere. And Lalio now seemed cheerful, though much more frail and insubstantial...while above us, there in the sky beyond the balcony, and then over the streets as well, an immense and pestilential woman—the poisoned reality of the day—continued to rush into the distance, brandishing her shears...

Once again I hear the wind beneath the door, and I cannot believe, without some special effort, that the pixie ever truly existed. I suppose (in the midst of tears) that the only life he ever knew was lived in the heavens of children—that splendid sky which lies over every Genoa. But then I discern an indescribable lament... the plaint of other Stellinos; and I conclude that the Follettos now on the earth are still quite numerous...or numberless. But here I'll return to recounting simple facts.

On the following day, October 10, same year, (I had spent the night in Genoa, after phoning my family in the outlying province and saying that the papers weren't yet ready and I'd have to wait), I returned—disturbed by the things I had seen, and perhaps incredulous—to the same snow-decked alley.

Perhaps I was hoping that the *house* (as happens in dreams) would no longer be there!

But it was. As dark and rickety as a cardboard set, and the mindless old man was stepping at that very moment through the door, cautiously, holding a shoe box under his arm.

On the balcony, high above (but from where she hadn't seen me), Ruperta thrust so far forward as to risk a fall and was following the figure of her lunatic brother with a painful sneer and a crazed intensity, as though counting his steps.

At a certain point she bellowed (in a voice I don't forget):

"Look at that paw! One of his paws is moving! You just be careful he doesn't run away!"

I was then to notice, with pained commiseration, that the box (emblazoned with the name of a well-known Genoa shoe store) had in fact been badly closed, and one of the legs of the tiny martyr peeped out from one its corners, and from another a small hairy forepaw, moving in uncertain imitation of the tender gestures of children as they wave good-bye to their mothers—a "*ciao, ciao, Mama!* " that would have moved any heart less stony and compressed by age than that of the Seamstress; but the gesture, really, was only a trick of the eye, because Stellino was dead.

I breathed a sigh of relief, though of sad relief.

Shortly afterwards, not very far from the house, the half-wit had found his way to the edge of the dump—where one surveyed a goodly portion of the broken pots, and scraps of dresses, and evil chronicles of world events which the Seamstress had left to accumulate there in the course of recent years—and having reached that spot, he dropped to his knees, smiling insipidly, placed the box on the snow, removed his beret...(Please God, let me pray that this is no dream) dribbled on the box a strand of spittle... Then he quickly removed its lid...

And what, here on our native soil, came out of it, if not—bright and light as three notes of joy—a bird... a happy skylark!

It rose trembling into the sky—which once again was azure, unadulterated May, decked with a necklace of almond blossoms—and vanished into the perfect purity of Creation.

All that remained on the ground was an empty shoe box, marked with the name of that well-known Genovese shoe store.

Unexpectedly, since the wind was blowing from the other direction, I again heard the bellowing voice of the Seamstress, first from the right, then from the left:

"Is he dead? Are you telling me the truth? He hasn't run off?"

"Dead!" replied the wind, rising light and suddenly, speaking for the poor harried half-wit with a voice exactly the same as his own, "Dead, my Sister, and buried!"

"And he's not to come back home tonight, *the old bit of rot*, with all his stupid demands!" the Seamstress once more cried.

"Rest easy! He'll never come home again! He's now in heaven," came the response, after a pause, of the half-wit's voice, drowsy and foolish, the words shot through with a kind of groan—and this time he spoke for himself.

But the wind, meanwhile—and who can say what ruffles up inside the wind, what voices of desperate children who are finally free, but always anxious again to cast their eyes on the mother who unjustly struck them?—within the wind there was a delicate voice which I seemed to recall; it rose and fell like the cry of a sightless kitten and finally complained:

"Ah, take me back! If only you knew how I love you,

my own dear Ruperta; how Stellino, your little star, loves his mother, how your own Folletto adores you. Don't you remember your baby, dear mother...that year of 1860... don't you, Mama, remember that spring, with Garibaldi and his soldiers?..."

I wanted to hear no more, and I left that place of snow and flowers, of wickedness and freedom, while saying to myself that the effect of love (the love of elves and half-wits) on the Universe itself, on the tremendous Reality of living a life, must indeed be strange and powerful when the air can begin to churn not only with the cries of children, but as well with the words of a Provençal poet, a Bernart de Ventadorn, or of a heart, like his, which is full of devotion.

The Great Street

Even today I remain perplexed by the simple-hearted abandon with which, as a child, I constantly returned to that great street. I can offer no precise idea of what clear motive might have prompted the girl I was—motive, or active sensation, or irrational urge—to turn that street, which coursed like an arid riverbed through the eastern part of the city, into the locus of her daily walks.

Clearly, however, that young girl's penchant for this ancient and exotic street was anything but natural, or even rational. Something much larger than myself, something of which I owned no possible realization, carried me there every day, as automatically as winds carry clouds, or as waves trail spray, or as night roams abroad with sleep and dreams.

Such a majestic, savage street! A river of rock; a colossal ship, anchored between banks of silence! A painting: a wonderful, melancholy composition that might have been entitled—like a canvas which glowed with mysterious life—"Freedom and Meditation"!

There was nothing in Naples to equal it. So strangely quiet yet animated, so open yet mysterious, it was one of the city's most solemn and wrongly neglected thoroughfares. No other place could have given the soul a finer sense of confusion and festivity, of bewilderment and joy, of freedom and fear; or could have billowed the mind with such delicate thoughts and veiled it with such painful, absentminded music. It carried the spirit, almost in flight, to the edges of a valley not shown on any of the maps of the world—to a place where the view opens out, incomparably calm and clear, onto the constant coming and going of eternal Symbols and staggering Ideas.

But like a queen cast out onto the ruin of a sidewalk, or like a sensitive woman forced to knock with silly ruses at the hearts of men, this unhappy street, which no one loved, seemed nearly to hope for a black-market purchase of the passer-by's attention—in exchange for a word that might soften a hostile, scattered mind—and decked itself at the start of its course with an ordinary, day-to-day attitude of bourgeois charm and gaiety: bright colors and sparkling smiles such as might have been found in the customary run of time-worn beauties. And along this stretch where its path began, just above the piazza that bears the name of Dante, people quite generally liked it. The red buildings, including the Museum's cheery facade, the small, green, gracious parks, the string of shops with their invitations to delightfully familiar purchases—everything helped to give it the air of an easy if somewhat boisterous grace. The sky's high clouds, sailing with swan-like calm in perfect azure; the nearly continuous tide of students, vociferous and gaily multicolored, to and fro from the nearby schools; the traffic of the carriages, the trolley-cars' clang, the wandering songs of the numerous minstrels; the recurrent sight of little old women selling violets and mums; the sequence, or more nearly the chase of cinema posters, red and blue, yellow and black, on the white, sun-washed walls: all of it seemed like a panoply of cries and joyful smiles cast off along its way by the handsome street. Banal, self-satisfied invitations. Yes, at its start in Piazza Dante and then for a lengthy stretch, this great street was nothing more than a vibrant, populous artery, a stream of traffic, simply a bit more lively than others would normally be.

But then came the hour when the day descends, almost imperceptibly, behind a dense horizon of city roofs and balconies, an hour when the light is almost always splendid; and if at that changing and somehow pensive hour which announces approaching evening, one allowed oneself the full embrace of such affectionate apparitions, obeying the heart's inclination to be carried away by the currents of long and populous thoroughfares, and therefore accepting the street's seductive invitations, then, on setting out between its banks, one realized, suddenly, with a twitch, that something about it had changed.

It had become a different street. No longer the one whose first bright stretch, at morning, had seemed so merry and reassuring. The fine, clear colors which had prodded the shamefully banal minds of the passers-by, and chipped a breech in their apathy, little by little were dying out, silently, on the buildings' taciturn faces. Which seemed more gray and distant. Facades were no longer gladdened by cheerful displays of sweets or colorful clothing stores; there were only cold closed doors, and windows stunned and ajar. The very crowd which shortly before had thronged the street had suddenly thinned, as though having taken flight. The students lagged far to the rear. The trolley cars, the carriages, the cars, the bicycles, the movie posters and the newspaper stands, the wandering musicians and the aged ladies plying mums and violets had likewise receded. The street had widened unexpectedly. Evening's arrival had made it a river of astonishing breadth. A charmed silence, like a cold flush of moonlight, loomed up from its furthest reaches and flew steadily forward along its banks, carrying shudders and presentiments of mournful, unknown beauty.

And then—as if the murmuring voices of the black trees, outlined in the distance at the sides of the street, or the gyrating wisps of bluish smoke, shaped like animals, queens, gallows and flowers, which someone sent constantly upward into that livid sky, were not enough; as if the alarming impression of a river's waters, provoked by the curious gleam of the cobblestones, might not have sufficed to create an air of bewitched expectation—strange things began to present themselves to the dazed observer's eyes. One began to grow aware of stores and tiny shops which during the day were of no particular interest; of faded displays of second-hand books, or of cages with birds, or of plaster cemetery sculpture. On the street's two banks—their lamps shining wan and astray in the darkness—incredible doors now filled with lights and scenes that were still less credible. Heroes, birds, and pale dead youths were the core of these night-time displays.

A sweet, putrid odor of crumbling paper issued from some of those shops. Illustrated magazines stood in piles at the sides of the doorways and served as pedestals for columns of likewise illustrated books that generations of children, burning with a pure and turbid joy, had passed back and forth from one to the other of their little hands. Many of those children were now no longer alive, or had grown up into corrupt adults, or in any case preserved no memory of those readings they once had loved. Yet those books and magazines survived. How the colors of their covers glowed in the whiteness of the moonlight! How naive and devoutly rhetorical were the faces of the heroes, the smiles and tears of the heroines! And how laden with calm and heartfelt beauty the landscapes in which they moved: lakes and forests, mountains and seas upon which the gazes of ancient schoolboys had lingered and strayed! The flags of all nations sparkled in the sun on the masts of brightly painted wooden ships that majestically entered and departed from the world's most famous ports and traveled the most distant seas. Young sailors with heads of curls like girls, and salty old pirates as dangerous and happy as eagles, sang and boozed around villainous tables in the yellow gleam of a lantern which shed more gloom than light on smoke-filled vaults where bats had built their hanging nests. Cliffs crowned by storm clouds and jolted by forks of lightning slightly more grandiose than natural plunged down onto dark and deserted beaches washed by a constant, roiling surge of long steely waves, topped with eerie shocks of spray. And those noises, those confused and alarmed voices of waves full of muted explosions—like frightened crowds in flight, or a train falling from a precipice, or the thunder of furious stampeding herds—set savage lights aglow in the eyes of Yann of the *Iceland Fishers*, sitting dazed and alone before that sea. Other more ingenuous personages, disquieted and delightfully menacing, here and there paced back and forth among these curious papers. Colonel Cody, on horseback, followed by a pack of red coyotes, finely painted, shaded his eyes with his hand and peered toward the hollow of a flaming canyon: framed at his back by an aery valley with the sparkling blue ribbon of a mountain stream, or the gleaming veil that drops from a waterfall's diadem, he attempts to espy the hidden, insidious movements of the advancing enemy. Bearded and attired in skins, the aging Robinson Crusoe shows an always magnificent bearing of courage and hope; with his prehistoric rifle over his arm, he walks through a perfect morning to hunt wild goats in the paradisiacal valleys of his Island, his eyes clouding over with regret for the loss of England and his much-loved mother as he watches the fineness of the sky. The *Explorers of the Deep* and the heroes of *Twenty Thousand Leagues Beneath the Sea* advance like ghosts, distraught, ecstatic, and forgetful of self in the midst of green tunnels dripping with water of the color of rubies and emeralds; they listen in primordial silence to fated songs of freely-running streams, of cool clear water that fills their throats and calms their terrible thirst. Gordon Pym, huddled on the floor of his dug-out boat as it tosses with neither light nor hope in the arms of an unknown sea, observes the approach, like an evil sun erupted from the floes of ice, of the Phantom of the Pole, knowing that soon it will devour him. When suddenly that terrifying landscape fades away. Canoes and clipper ships, pirogues and colorful junks carried their passengers down the rivers and along the coasts of all the most exotic lands, beneath the most favorable suns and winds. The world of youthful adventures mingled with the world of the passions, the joys of discovery with the joys of dreams, the pleasures of smiles with the finer frenzy of tears, expressing the desire to step beyond the truths of everyday and to grasp something newer and far more daring. The youthful heroes on the Paris barricades—the sun and fury of the South, mixed with the virginal freshness of Nordic blood—died with foreheads wreathed in splendor beneath the volleys of Bonapartist rifles. Cosetta gave her hand to Dea. Ghastly Quasimodo perished while cavorting on the edge of the abyss, in the immense music of Notre Dame, just as the sailor perishes in a vast clamor of the waves. The happy and vibrant youthfulness of the *Three Musketeers* pelted fistfuls of light into the darkness of the Paris streets. One world shed its light on another; a caravan of images prepared the most suitable road, the most suggestive lights, for the ones that followed. Now comes the throng of *David Copperfield*, Mr. Micawber at its head, laughing and crying in the midst of his numerous offspring while climbing the gangway to the immigrant-laden deck of the boat which will finally take him to Australia, far from the horrors and delights of debtors' prison. Here are all the members of the Pegotty family, seated around the table of the fine Yarmouth houseboat while the fascinating Steerforth, still unaware of what his much-tried heart will decide, listens thoughtfully and attentively to the artless talk of Cam and Little Emily. Beyond the tiny windows, the sea slants out in evening desolation and voices its bewildered horror of all the events which are still to come. Germanic phantoms, painfully universal, throw open the doors to a world of truth and splendor. Ysolte caresses her plaits in the light of the moon. Young Werther walks absorbed among the alleys of his ancient city. Portraits of Schubert and Beethoven are so intense as to seem to show a hundred men in a single face. And then, suddenly, everything changes: the landscape, the sky, the tone of the times. Images arose from a space a thousandfold more ample than reality: Cossacks, Napoleon at Jena, tundra, Moscow covered with snow. Who might these men have been, so shabby and tired, but bearing faces that shone with immortal goodness and joy? The hoary head of the great Leon, husband to Sophia Andreievna, gleamed weakly in the gray air, against the grimy walls of Astopov's station where he waited, after telling the story of the earth, to depart for the skies. In the midst of tattered and afflicted rabble, madmen and boys, angelic princes and guileless monsters, Dostoievski shattered his chains; his suddenly resplendent hands, in the infinite gray of this prison which comprises the whole of the earth, were the pure, liberating hands of Christ himself. Chekov, careless of the fearful rat which nourished itself on his lungs, recounted ironic fables of a bourgeois Russia, but his gaze from time to time slipped thoughtfully behind a wall: beyond it, shining in the pink of the moonlight, his venerable Cherry Orchard, the place where the winds of by-gone days go to die.

It's likely that, in the morning, a few innocent children or wandering students from time to time would stop enchanted before these shops, pondering a trade of the scant coins in their pockets for one of those books from the covers of which so many slightly sad but marvelous figures peered out at them. But then they would go away, and no one else would arrive for the rest of the day. Only the rain or the wind, the sun or the clouds in the turquoise sky offered a delicate consolation to those aging papers and ancient stories. A silence, or an air of endless meditation, or the tone of some forgotten song collected on those sidewalks, before those well-worn thresholds. Surely it was clear that the goals pursued by the owner or owners of those shops went far beyond all normal pecuniary interest. One hardly opens a shop in a desert; one doesn't create displays for an audience of clouds and paving stones. So those shops, as far as I could see, had to be theaters of Memory; they were part of a series of Signs and Symbols through which that ancient, contemplative street provided itself with a representation of the senseless beauty of living; of the dreams of the youngsters who came to visit it during the day—those youngsters whose light-footed paces, alas, were only briefly the same.

And then, when the passer-by's fancy already had been pierced and perturbed by these apparitions, other scenes began to advance with ever waxing urgency. Whether their indistinct whiteness derived from the light of the moon or from the absence of blood in the veins of the figures composing them is something I could not say. But the shops full of stories and birds lay ever further behind them.

No lights shone at all in these tiny stores, of far poorer aspect than the ones before.

I had been told that modest artisans worked in those shops by day and crafted figures of youths: statues, medallions, and plaster busts with which to adorn the tombs of Departed Students, long or but recently dead, who lay within the cemetery nearby.

No one, however, could relieve me of the thought that those figures in white stone or plaster were something far more alive than effigies.

The blood, yes, had abandoned their veins, but not so long ago. These bodies remained still warm and charged with sleepy dreams.

The good artisan, who as sunset approached had been anxious to sit down at table with his sons, had left some of them unfinished and they lay about the floor, tiredly resting on a flank, with a hand beneath a cheek, just as in life those students at times had fallen asleep over a difficult problem or a tedious exercise in Latin. Curls no longer brown or blond, but the color of snow and eternal old age, fell across a temple; eyes were wide and empty, since their pupils had been stolen by headlong time. One group of these students, entirely naked, as though just risen from their beds, formed a hedge of slender bodies and eager, enraptured, downward-looking faces around a young companion who, seated and holding an open book on his thin knees, seemed intent on reading who knows what fables or vibrant poems. His mouth was half open, but his eyes were empty, except that a few drops of tears, likewise in plaster, ran down from their corners and across his delicate cheek. With the back of his other hand (such a very fine hand) he wiped them away.

Other figures held a foot just barely raised from the earth, and seemed to be taking leave of some cherished threshold while casting an affectionate backward glance, perhaps to a mother or to much-loved brothers and friends who waved good-bye. All around, on high, crude shelves, were small garlanded heads of younger boys: some gazed joyously upwards to invisible suns, others cast smiling glances at the charms of a lovely garden, another looked in timid enchantment at a sky to which soon he would have to bid farewell. Still another saw nothing at all; leaning slightly back on a shoulder, with a tiredness barely heavier than that of a boy in the first year of his studies, he seemed to be resting.

One group struck me with particular force: it stood at the threshold of one of these shops and portrayed a twelve-year-old schoolboy. A lovely young woman led him by the hand and pointed out a path that remained invisible to those who stood outside in the street. The young woman's lips were slightly parted, and surely her words were wise and kind, her promises prompt with consolation. So, why, pulling back from that compassionate caress, distraught and bewildered by a pain too intense for tears, did he turn his face toward the door and cast his avid gaze out of that vast silent room, in hopes of seeing someone who might be rushing to his aid? It seemed that rivers and mountains and crystalline waters, turquoise skies and wind-blown trees with rustling boughs, and days spent running on the hill... and luminous repose and blessed maternal caresses, and home and school and unruffled childhood all lay on the other side of the threshold he had crossed; and that they called him, and he wanted with all his heart to return to them, to his fond, now-abandoned Life. But already the pupils of his eyes had dried and vanished, and his hand—owing perhaps to a lack of attention on the part of the mason who had shaped it, or perhaps for some deeper, more terrible reason—the fingers, alas, of that delicate schoolboy's hand, which lifted to entreat those sacred gifts, were missing; his hand was a skeletal stump and could no longer grasp or hold onto anything.

No outside noise or light had the power to shake these unhappy students from their sad immobility and desperate calm. The books they read, their dreams, smiles, good-byes, and tears, everything about them now had the air of finality, suspension, eternal fixity.

It was here, one felt, rather than anywhere else, that the beat of the great street's heart pulsed at its most majestic, most intimate, most spiritual and distressed.

These doors, these displays, were followed by no others.

Via Foria—the name of this great street—slipped away toward the gray recesses of the Botanical Gardens; away as well, it seemed, toward an even vaster park; away like a voyager too exhausted by the morning's wonders, the midday songs, and the evening's melancholy sweetness to be able now to look forward to anything more than a quiet stroll, free from even the palest of memories.

Redskin

Just three years ago, when my brother Manuele was still alive, the most beautiful room in our house, the room in the corner towards the port, had no real furniture. Its only trappings were cots and wooden crates, and I could dream this dream which strikes me now as mournful and absurd.

So: a sailing ship called *Maria Rosaria*, one of the many which used to dock beneath our windows loading up barrels; spectacular spankers, and planking old but good. On board this docile house my older brother and I would go sweetly sailing, first skirting the coast of Sorrento, then down off-shore toward Sicily, and afterwards, seasoned by months of navigation, out onto the open oceans of the world, like the Atlantic or the mind's smiling Pacific. He was to captain the ship, and I, equipped with German paints from home, was to paint the landscapes and the colorful peoples of those places, indulging my greatest passion.

"But would it take a lot to buy it (the boat)?" I inquired.

This nervous young man with his Arab head and full violent lips, his upraised arms held blocked in mid-air as he paused in the practice of his semaphore signals (we had little flags of every color), looked at me with a smile:

"Sure it will, but the important thing is for me to get my papers"—his masters' papers as a small craft captain—"so I can start to sail a bit, and then we'll see."

Returning to his semaphore signals, plying his muscular limbs, he gently sang a phrase of the *"Hinno de la Libertad,"* which was our favorite:

Libertad, haz que dulce resuene....

These things can seem comical, but they were real and true: our passion, our fledgling hope. But my heart languished from the bitterness, already then, of a hardly veiled derision to which Manuele and I, from some time back, were subjected by our more civil brothers who went to the upper schools. I also knew the melancholy—from which my brother suffered less—of our plans' implausibility, at least for the time being; and beside it, as well, the vague but every day more forceful distress of witnessing the swell and hearing the rising din everywhere around us of contemporary civilization: it pressed in upon us and entered our lives with the very breathing of our brothers, no less than with the slippery yet stubborn necessity to chart some solid, sedentary future among the local population. And rumors already had begun to spread about the banishment of all those splendid *Maria Rosarias* from beneath the windows of the house, and on the probable demise of the red lighthouse, and of gorging the waters of the port with land-fill. This quarter at the edge of the port was scheduled to disappear, with all its belfries, and fish-mongers, and jovial poverty. So there was no time to lose: the two of us had to set to work to find the ship we needed, to embark with colorful pennants and German paints and fine aspirations onto the paths of adventure and salvation, weighing anchor toward the lands of freedom. But we never spoke about such things at home, where the others would have reproved us dourly. It was a secret. Unaware of the coming end to their world, the ancient seagulls, amidst confusions of sails and the palpitation of waters, clouds, and wind, meanwhile squawked their candid poetry.

One morning I said:

"We should decorate our room, what do you say?" (to my brother Manuele).

Intent on whittling an arrow from a stick of wood, he looked up at me. I made no immediate mention of the name, since I feared that my intimate feelings, my silent and original love, might be read on my face: that name was White Horse. So I did not speak it. But, holding my chin in my hand, I suggested:

"How about my painting a life-size Redskin, and then tacking him up above the cot? Just imagine the impression it would make, on entering the room!"

But it wasn't that I wanted to show off. For some months past I had read reports in certain missionary pamphlets deploring the decline of the wonderful American tribes we so much loved, which had left me deeply disturbed. I showed no interest in my food, I was listless and moped about, my only solace was the headlong discussion I daily tabled with the family on "the white man's treachery," and other such exaggerations. They didn't much listen to me, which moreover didn't much bother me, since my constant, pressing anxieties lay elsewhere. I was writing (just imagine!) a book: a novel (though surely far superior to the usual brand of adventure tales) in which I intended to present the tragedy of the last Red Indian: a Sioux and the only survivor still afloat on the white tide which had engulfed the world: despised, hunted down, and so forth. A book that would make a great impression, though in an utterly superior way. At least that much was clear to me. Yet my Hero's misadventure had been double: in addition to his natural woes, I had summoned him to the city of New York, where owing to my wholly deficient knowledge of the city's plan and topography he had gotten definitively lost. And the only thing to do with my excursion into literature was to give it up, leaving me at the mercy of a higher emotional fever than I might have ever feared. The Hero, the Hero! Compared with my Hero, the whole complex world that bustled all around me seemed only a tired old man napping in an easy chair; and no analogy more depressing could be imagined. It smothered and oppressed me like a descending fog. How could I flee, where could I reach him, what free roads of the world could I travel to encounter the last of the Heroes?

All of this somehow helps to explain my ever so daring decision: to turn to my colored pencils, and on quite a grand scale. No matter how paltry and ineffective, my pencils were in fact the only remaining means through which I could hope to recreate my noble friend and to have him present at my side. But first, I wanted the approval of my brother Manuele. He was the expert in all such matters; I needed to know whether or not my plans in art were a good idea. And he nodded endorsement, though still I remember the curious smile beneath his heavy eyelashes.

So we set out together, I myself quite feverishly, and found a sheet of wrapping paper almost half the height of the wall. After spreading it out on the floor of that empty room and kneeling down on top of it (there was no other way to deal with it), I set nervously to work, turning for my model to a print I owned of a Redskin before the advent of civilization. As my efforts progressed, cries of wonder issued from my lips, broken sounds of excitement and commotion. White Horse was appearing before our eyes, as though rising up through the floor, his head two times the size of my own, his lips clamped shut down close to his chin, his eyes half-closed in a squint and extremely powerful; he wore a crown of feathers three feet tall, and arms of a similar length lay folded across his chest. My Hero's voluminous face was then to be shaded in with red, and as soon as I had finished I balled up my fists to contain the joy that flooded all the way to my frenzied fingertips. I gazed at the figure in utter rapture, expressing my commotion with reckless ardor and declaring the devotion I would always show him. My brother Manuele, who had paced back and forth across the room and never for a moment abandoned me, was likewise stunned: bending down to look at my work, he laughed with delight.

"The feathers," I cried, "how should I do the feathers?"

He offered advice by touching various pencils: mainly the greens and yellows. But turquoise too, and black, were also fine, with a blood-red splash here and there.

Then on to the final touches.

When the beacon ignited and rhythmically spilled its light into the room through the bluish panes of glass, I had finished. With four nails and my brother's help, I quickly raised the Hero to the space on the wall above the cot, in place of a few saints' images (quite yellowed) which I reverently removed. He instantly stood on his feet, his giant torso erect (twice any normal size), his head steady, his eyes half-closed. Proudly he surveyed us: as though tied to the stake for torture, but indifferent to adverse destiny.

His arm was draped with a yellow cloth, and behind it fell the last vast light of sunset, the prairies growing somber with shadowed gullies. We lit a candle in our room. With hearts full of passionate devotion, we gazed at him.

But a few days later—and some of the reason may have lain in my other brothers' gibes—a kind of anguish rose darkly up inside me, and then I descried its source in my intuition of something somehow exaggerated which rayed from all my primitive colors. I was taken as though by the first shiver of a chill, faced with the objective, disconcerting projection of my passion. As soon as I had grasped this fact, I grew quite pale and would have wanted immediately to destroy my work: its presence seemed unbearable. My God, what had I done? My Hero's colossal naiveté—he stood there erect, absorbed in all his thoughts, unapprised of how wrongly I had rendered him—sent a dark tremor into my heart, a taste of tears, and I remained transfixed by a feeling of enormous pity for his fate. He could not know how wrong he was, that his noble stance was charged with self-contradiction. My pain lay in knowing that I myself had thrown him so carelessly into such a plight, from a lightness of love. I spent whole hours of fervent analysis before him, and then, having found no possible remedy, would heave a sigh and leave the room, so as not to be wholly overwhelmed by the tenderness that my Hero's gaze—heavy, pained and disdainful—was able to arouse within me. I loved him desperately, and couldn't have denied it. Yet the more this feeling grew, the more my conscious mind, as though from somewhere outside of me, plagued me with a sense of the ridiculous, of his grotesque lack of verisimilitude, of the absurdity of his presence in a house like ours—that bourgeois home of white-collar workers and high-school students. The very dimensions of the painting, which invaded half the room, aroused a fearful presentiment of others' sarcastic misgivings on my state of mind, which already was fairly obvious.

"But don't you get the feeling," I asked my brother Manuele, who was always kind and encouraging, "that there's something excessive about this picture?" He replied, "Of course not, he looks absolutely real." But these words came absent-mindedly, since Manuele's eye was fastened on certain ships in the offing beyond the lighthouse, boats which might grant him those papers to which I've referred, our common dream. So his words came absent-mindedly.

Immediately afterwards, hoping at least to attenuate, no matter how slightly, the strange impression that the solitary Hero excited in whomever entered the room, I set to painting another sheet of wrapping paper, same size as the first, with the image of a group of Mexican Revolutionaries on horseback, in a courtyard lit by sooty lanterns.

Such terrifying faces. One of these men, whom I had already encountered in Galopin, was truly capable of frightening me, perhaps because he bent his head in my direction. That was why I tried while painting not to look at him; instead I directed lofty thoughts of fidelity toward the giant Sioux, and frequently turned devoted eyes to gaze at him. So how can I explain? When the Rebel had planted his feet into his stirrups, his air grew compelling and victorious, and he stared at me unceasingly. I was forced, as though by some greater power, to treat him better than the others, most especially setting him off with a fine vermilion scarf wrapped almost like a serpent around his waist, which he accepted with satisfaction. The others then seemed to bend dark and indignant faces towards their breasts and observed me with reproach; I was forced to make vermilion scarves for all of them. And finally, after asking that I doff his sombrero and enable him to salute me, the Chief invited me to follow him and join the group. Another horse, with powerful flanks and a parti-colored saddle, was waiting in the courtyard. They would ride through the wilds of Mexico, spreading revolt against ugly and invasive civilization. Why didn't I join them? "If only you would come!" they thundered and groaned in their native tongue, while raising their doll-like yet splendid rifles as a sign of greeting. I heard them sing the much loved verse:

Libertad, haz que dulce resuene

and tears of reverent ecstasy ran down my face.

Where now are all these Heroes, and why didn't I go away with them?

Maybe I didn't go with away them since, after a first moment of magnificent wonder, I ever more clearly discerned in them the same faults of construction which already had afflicted me in White Horse. I wasn't yet able to comprehend the poetry, indeed the logic of such mistakes: meaning that, yes, these Heroes were badly drawn and lacking in verisimilitude, but this was precisely their greatest virtue, since technical perfection always marks the final decay of the worlds in which Heroes live. The heroic is but barely roughed out, gigantic, boisterous, fundamentally awry, and, more than anything else, unspoiled by calculated aestheticisms. I grasp this only now.

Yet all the same, even while shy of accepting the Rebels' proposal, I couldn't get the better of the sense of veneration (indeed, I surrendered to it) which all of them, from White Horse to each and every one of the Rebels, aroused in me. Lively interior discussions in which I argued the pros and cons of corrections here and there (here the feathers didn't look quite right, there the Chief had too boyish an arm) would conclude with my throwing myself with half-closed eyes onto the cot to contemplate them all, delighting in their silent songs, spinning stories on their private lives, on the ways they had lived out the day, on the particular scenes of passionate nobility or ferocity in which some one of them had most particularly shone.

All sorts of things would go through my mind. But my deepest and most tender feelings were always reserved for White Horse, owing perhaps to the very same charge of melancholy which filled me with pity for him; or possibly—this is what I am more inclined to believe—because of that forceful air of primitivism which exuded from his image, often to the point of transfiguring its visible flaws (as only the passage of the years was later conclusively to do). Here, yes, was a human being: a true man: colossal, out of kilter, ingenuous, ferocious and sad: just as it is with all that race of savages in whom the passions, finding no outlet in expeditious reasoning, remain imprisoned in their eyes, like the deep, pain-filled eyes of animals. He was a creature I could truly love. He was beautiful.

So these were my favorite friends. And then came the time of my life—and of the life of the corner room towards the port—when White Horse and the Rebels-in-arms were followed by a great long train of barbarous men, amid a gaggle of women and boys, who seemed in high agitation to demand repair of their forced imprisonment, their unsolicited banishment. Raven hair-dos of *caballeros*, and mantillas of *señoras*, and bleakly scowling *niños* peered out from sheets of wrapping paper of more or less respectable size, and from smaller sheets as well, or even indeed from pages whisked from high-school students' notebooks. Horses, servant girls, bandits, beggars, wild beasts, caves with a harsh wood table and a candle, sinister scenes in the dark, or windy vistas with flashes of sunlight, with scudding clouds and receding hills, and of course the mandatory horses mounted by riders with rifles: these images and themes overflowed the walls of the room, which showed not a single patch of unoccupied space. Anyone who peered through that door on a stormy day received quite a strange impression. The wind whistled in various cracks, the watery horizon throbbed pale and disturbed on the window panes to the rear, and on every side that vast extravagant multitude seemed to leap forward, dark and full of suspicion, as though issuing from the wooden crates or springing from the cots: *¡Voto a Dios! hola! hola!* (their native language being Spanish.) They were cause for understandable dismay. And I myself loved all of them, in spite of chagrin for my draftsmanship, and in spite of my brothers' ever more pointed derision. Now I think back with special nostalgia to the lavish costume with which I outfitted one figure: the fastidious Don Jaime, a sort of Peruvian prince who from that day onward always observed me with kindness, silently, crossing one leg over the other. I recall the Wise Old Man, a Pilgrim whom I had thought to introduce to my first Hero, my Indian. And so many others, so very many. Ordinary life had ceased to hold any meaning for me, I hardly understood it at all, and a single silent spasm beleaguered me day by day, with ever mounting intensity: the desire to abandon that room and to flee far away into the glorious lands of the Heroes. And even while never saying so, I lay my pallid hopes all the more exclusively upon my brother Manuele, who unlike the others had preserved his freedom from all contemporary bondage, and who knew, sitting with his face towards the sea, how to sing.

But this, precisely, was the moment in which my world began to draw to a close. One morning I was forced to realize that my brother Manuele was no longer there. He had walked down the lane to the port and had signed for a berth on one of those ships at anchor beside the lighthouse, briskly embarking for the lands of the Heroes—as he had always thought to do—and from there he'd bring back the boat which was vitally important to both of us, a brig, or a schooner, or whatever else.

I had no hopes except in him. But then, whenever he returned, he always seemed more spent and dazed, almost as though, perched among the masts, he were looking beyond the sea and watching the escape before his eyes of the golden coast we had dreamed of together, as though the flying jibs and spankers and fluttering stuns'ls of our own *Maria Rosaria* had been carried away in the force of the final storm. Now, when I talked about the plans which once had been so dear to us, he no longer replied, "The important thing is for me to get my papers." Instead, while massaging his thumbs against his red ropy hands, he would look at me as though returning from a heavy dream, still lost in one of those moments when words at first don't quite make sense. Little my little, I ceased to question him at all. Timidly, I would simply remind him in my letters of some of the things we once had talked about. Had he changed his mind, perhaps?

All my other brothers, the sensible ones, meanwhile had grown adult and authoritarian, and there came the point when they were no longer willing to confront, upon entering that wonderful room, those great sheets of painted paper and that strange and unbecoming population of disquieting figures and faces. They had the wooden crates carried away, declared the cots an eyesore, and discussed what might be best in the way of new furniture, which promptly arrived. Then came the walls: the general hustle and bustle of untacking my barbarous tribe, which lustily cried rebellion in their native Spanish (or so I seemed to hear in my desperation) and struck up strains of war, voicing our favorite song:

Ciudadanos, volad a las armas,
repeled repeled la opresión.

The soul's vain longing.... All of them were stripped away from me, carried off who knows where, leaving my heart in bloody tatters.

And the Sioux, as he descended, owing perhaps to the buckling of the paper, bent his mammoth head to his breast, which is a detail I always remember. It gripped me with uncontainable anguish, almost as though he had signaled a final gesture of farewell, intended only for me, who so greatly had loved him, always.

Ciudadanos, volad a las armas,

all of them now seemed to sob; whereas the Indian, having slipped a feather between his teeth, slowly descended from the wall with the supreme sardonic peace of his race.

Dear White Horse. I was never to see him again.

A few months later—months of desperate solitude and a weeping heart, and as well of the weight of my now evident worthlessness in coping with the problems of practical life, the life of modern civilization—I learned that I had taken permanent leave of my brother Manuele too. And in spite of fervent hopes, he in fact was never to return again: lengthy hours spent waiting in front of the casements facing the sea were rewarded by no new glimpse of that familiar dark profile as it slipped with a wave through the gate, nor of the mast of his ship shivering on the windowpanes. Such news resembles a strange new spring which passes through the air with songs of love and fatal oblivion for the ones already passed. The lighthouse no longer holds its own, and collapses; the sailing ships go off to weep in seclusion, and the windows call out to them in vain, that at least the pain be shared. But no, they don't return. Workers come instead, and feats of engineering reshape the port, filling in these waters with blocks of stone; over there a formidable edifice conceals the blue of the sky; over here, everything demolished, rebuilt, changed.

All of which, of course, is necessary, and I make no complaint about its fatal advance, its joyful headstrong breathlessness. Necessities. Human necessities.

But how, now, can I hope for some *Maria Rosaria* to make her way through these shallow waters, tangled with debris?—a *Maria Rosaria* with a host of colorful pennants, and come to take me far away, as once I tenderly awaited, trusting in her alone: innocent deliverance and blessed liberation.

It may seem strange, but I can't help awaiting her arrival. Indeed, on certain peaceful evenings, I find myself surprised by the light tap, the wing of this gull against the windowpane. But it makes no more than the very gentlest sound, nearly imperceptible, almost as though of a spiritual substance which could call no more strongly. Begging all real things, and work, to wait a while, I find myself aboard the boat; an empty boat, its shrouds intoning happy hopes, invoking the land of the Heroes. And that land is there. I disembark, and the Heroes carouse around me on great swift horses. Here they have found a place where civilization has not followed them, and their powerful mouths sing hymns of peace and rediscovered joy, the light of endless sunset fleeing behind them, outlining hooves and tall hats.

Which, of course, is a dream.

Yet this turning back, if only for a moment or so, is good: the freedom, pleasure, and sometimes tears of returning to the melancholy, once-loved heroes, and to White Horse; and to my brother Manuele, and so many others.

The Villa

When I had become rich, extremely rich, after so many years in which I had written an endless number of graceful inventions, I went to wash my face and my hands, which were all black with ink, before going down to purchase for my Princess *all the things I had to purchase.* Then, this fine December morning, I went to her house to visit her.

I couldn't have been more nervous. At the time when I had said good-bye to her to go off and into the world, she had been living in Via dei Tre Fanali, No. 43, the second street off Corso Umberto. Things when I had left had been in quite a mess, but I would never have imagined, on returning, to find myself faced with a state so close to total ruin. The street was abandoned, deserted, the building a shambles. I descended from my lovely carriage, which I hitched with a ribbon to a post, and my eyes roved upward to survey the facade, which stood seven storeys tall. Not a living soul in sight. I looked for the concierge. She wasn't there.

"Excuse me, does the Princess still live here?" I inquired of a little boy who appeared as I was mounting the stairs.

"Yes, Miss," he replied respectfully. "Sometimes I

take her carnation buds that I find along the road, but she doesn't pay me very well."

I smiled with luscious satisfaction. Very well and good. Now I'm here to take care of things.

"Have you seen the carriage in the street?" I asked the child.

"The one with the small white horses, all gold, and with the dome?"

"That one. It's mine. Bye-bye."

Happy at having ruffled him a bit, I ran up the flights of stairs, reached the sixth floor, found a small black door, pushed against it, and then saw light. In the light there emerged an incredibly shabby easy chair, and the woman napping in the easy chair was poor, but with an air of something capricious and bizarre. Her features were fine, but haggard, her hair gray and thin. A cat curled up on her lap (a strangish kitten) regarded me with pained hostility. On the wall was a portrait of a sad young man. At the window, on the brightly lit sill, there sat a scarlet cluster of geraniums.

"Mama!" I cried, embracing her.

She awoke and smiled.

"I've come back from very far away," I explained. "How are you feeling?"

"So, so," she said, "I always think about Manuele."

She pointed at the little picture in which I recognized, without surprise (and soon you'll see for what happy reasons), my brother who had been a sailor, and who had died mysteriously at the age of twenty.

"And the others?" I asked.

"Married."

"So you always live alone?"

"I say my prayers to the Lord. I have these geraniums. And this lovely cat"—she kissed it—"who keeps me such good company. Don't you remember Anima?"

The cuddly, gray cat, which had been my true, great passion as a girl, surveyed me with eyes so deep and desperate, sarcastic and disdainful, that a shiver ran straight through me, and I planted a hearty, impulsive kiss on its tiny rubbery nose.

"I've always been just crazy about him," the Princess assured me, holding him up all soft and awry in both of her hands, to rub him against her cheek.

"All in all, then, you're happy?"

"Dear," she replied, "I hope the Lord will finally take me into His kingdom, where I'll find Manuele again, and not be alone any more, and I'll have lots of flowers. They're so expensive, so terribly expensive!..." she concluded, somewhat bitterly. And then, with a smile: "...and where my little Anima too will have gingerbread cookies to eat, and a pretty little dish full of milk."

Dear Mama. My eyes brimmed with tears. How hard I had struggled, and for so many years, to be able to give her what she wanted, *everything she wanted*... But now that everything was ready, I could hardly manage, myself, to believe it.

"Mama," I suddenly began, "would you come away with me?"

"But where, at this late date?"

"I have a villa."

"A villa? You?"

"Yes, me. A big, new villa. With a garden. There are wonderful surprises."

"Oh God, and how did you get it?"

"I wrote books full of wonderful stories, delicate and very pure, just the way you wanted... Streams, flowers, angels...you know, very old fashioned..."

"And you were thinking of me?"

"But of course!" I affirmed as I hugged her again while Anima, lying on his back in her lap, squirmed about in a fit of pique. "You've always been the very first thought in my mind, always. Why do you think I worked so hard? Come on, Mama, get up and come away with me. This is happiness."

She now seemed overcome by a great, incredulous joy.

"You...then you really love me? Oh Lord, let me thank you!" she exclaimed, drying her tears and joining her hands.

I helped her rise to her feet.

"I'll come as I am," she said timidly. "I don't own a hat anymore."

She walked to the windowsill to pick up the vase of geraniums and pressed it against her breast, and then, with Anima squirming in the crook of her arm, she descended the flights of stairs with me. As she went, her eyes charged with tears of tenderness and remorse, she lovingly kissed those ancient walls, which, she said, "had seen her passing through." I wasn't at all surprised. Anima, burdened with his heavy thoughts, had closed his eyes and lay snuggled against her shoulder.

I will never forget my mother's cry, after a trip of three days and three nights through marvelous cities and enormous forests, when our golden carriage stopped in a solitary plain, before a garden surrounded by a high white wall. Entering, she suddenly heard the voices of a thousand gold and purple birds singing brightly among the boughs of orange trees; she saw the villa, and the sailor who approached her.

She went quite stiff.

He was right before her, and took her into his arms.

"Now you mustn't cry," Manuele said, tall, swarthy-skinned and with his wonderful smile in his proud, bright eyes. "Everything's all over now, everything's alright."

But the poor Princess could take no more. She sobbed and sobbed. I smiled in Manuele's direction, knowing how he felt. He too was moved. The birds, meanwhile, sang more intensely, and some of them, full of daring, began to emerge from the shrubbery to see who was there. They skimmed through the pure blue sky like bubbles of soap. Dozens of them circled around her head. One of them, all red and—strangely—with a wingtip tinged in blue, settled on her shoulder and unabashedly kissed her ear, declaring his desire to have a talk with her. The others bubbled with laughter.

"Good Lord," the Princess said, caressing it and finally shaking free of her lapse into tears. "This bird just kissed me."

"They're all like that," Manuele explained.

"He no longer shoots at them with a slingshot," I joked.

He smiled.

"How fine, how truly fine!" my mother exclaimed. "Ah, dear son!" and she hugged him again.

That point marked the appearance, advancing from the depths of the park, of a great oval of light, between white and vermilion.

My mother uttered a cry, and remained enchanted.

"Who *is* that?" she asked in a thick, tremulous voice.

The light came forward, and in the midst of it, perfectly drawn, we saw Jesus himself, dressed in white, his red worker's cape folded double over his shoulder, his hazel hair well combed, his forehead calm and open, his eyes serene, his bearing frank and gentle.

"It's me," he said with a smile.

"You, Lord!? Here?" she cried, beside herself, dropping to her knees with the two of us right next to her.

(Anima, quite disgusted, had leapt to the ground.) Poor Mama. She didn't realize, in so delectable a moment, that even while turning a mien of affectionate benevolence—of infinitely loving benevolence—towards her and the youthful sailor, the Lord nonetheless gave no sign at all, unfortunately, of taking account of me. And for that he had his own good reasons.

"Lord," she continued with joyous exuberance, "I don't know how to thank you. Will I always be able to stay here? Always? You've given Manuele back to me. There are so many beautiful trees. And the birds, you know, they already know me, really. Tell him, Manuele. My daughter, Anna, tells me she has made a lot of money. But how is it possible to buy all this, in the kind of times we live in?"

"That's something you're not to bother about," Jesus replied, as he took the cat into his arms. Anima looked at him with dark and quarrelsome eyes, and attempted to scratch him. "Is this your cat?" he asked.

"Oh, yes. Give him your blessing. Be good, Anima, can't you see that this is the Lord? And will you too, Lord, always live here?"

"Of course."

"But…who brought you here?… What…what can I have done?"

Again the poor Princess was quite perturbed.

"Daughter," Jesus began, while caressing the contentious little beast ("You mustn't scratch," my mother scolded), "a small soul far more naughty than this cat"—"Oh, forgive me!" my mother exclaimed, extending her trembling arms to take the creature back, but Jesus didn't release him and Anima softly cried "meow…meow" while I myself went red, mortally distraught with anger—"gave me enormous sums of charity for the poor. That's why I live here. And also, I very much like you."

"It's best to give her the cat," Manuele said with a smile, seeing how flustered and anxious the Princess felt. Jesus placed it in her arms and surveyed her with affection.

My eyes had filled with sad and prideful tears, and, to hide them, I turned and looked off into the distance; I gazed at a red pavilion, in Chinese style, toward the rear of a lateral avenue, close to the wall of the park, and in front of this pavilion there shone another light, this time blue, pacing calmly back and forth. I was spellbound. The Mother of God had come out for a turn on the threshold. Quite an elegant little figure. Her veil of pale blue silk shadowed her narrow black eyes, her red mouth, her smiling face, and one of her hands held a charming little parasol, white and open in the sun. In the other hand was a tiny watering can, painted green, and she was using it, among the heavy shadow of the chestnut trees, to water the pink geraniums in one of her flower beds. The shimmer of her silver, three-pointed crown and her rosary blended with the sparkling streams of water. After a while she returned inside.

During the first few days the Princess couldn't contain herself, for joy and gratitude. She would have wanted us all, as well as the cat, to sleep at the foot of the Red Pavilion, wholly unmindful of the humid nighttime air, so as always to be close, she said, to the Lord and his gracious young Mother. But together we managed, especially this latter, to dissuade her.

"No, dear. As a favor to me. I want you to do as I say. Just look, such a lovely villa."

"But Ma'am, your Majesty, it's not the place where you are..."

No, but...well, I always keep my eye on it. Here... take this carnation shoot..."

"Will it root?"

"If you water it well, yes. It's a rather special variety, with petals that come to a point..."

"How kind of you, Ma'am! Manuele, just look at what a lovely queen we have. Kneel down, Anna."

We knelt. Manuele kissed the Queen's hand; I myself feigned absentmindedness. Kneeling down like that was something I wouldn't have wanted to do.

"And now, Ma'am, we'll be off and won't bother you anymore."

"Bother? But what a thing to say! You must come whenever you like. And, children, you're not to upset her."

Jesus, seated at a table, was making supper of a little bread and cheese and a glass of milk, and he was looking in our direction.

"Bye-bye, Sir!"

We walked beneath the turquoise sky, in the hot velvety air, and made our way happily back to the villa through the golden grove of orange trees. But we were greeted by an ugly surprise. Anima, that awful cat, came leaping down the steps with a little purple bird in its mouth.

"Oh, my God!" exclaimed the poor Princess, dashing to the rescue. "My God, no! One of the Lord's little birds! Save it! Otherwise I'll die of embarrassment!" We rescued the creature in the nick of time, Anima scampered away, and the luckless little bird, crazy with rage but once again, if shakily, on its feet, screamed "cheep cheep cheep" while spreading its two small wings and repeatedly throwing its mouth wide open, clearly demanding justice.

"Oh, you poor little thing, forgive me; I'm so terribly sorry!" came the Princess' supplication.

But the creature wouldn't hear of it, and continued,

trembling with rage, to squeal thousands of reproofs at the now absconded cat.

Manuele laughed.

"Mama," I attempted to persuade her, "but what's to beg pardon about? This place belongs to you. I paid for it. The Lord, along with the Queen, is a guest. Don't you see?"

She dried her tears.

"It just doesn't seem possible."

"But that's how it is."

The villa—I've forgotten to describe it—was very beautiful. A whole succession of smallish rooms, tapestried with flowered wallpaper, and with smallish windows no more than three feet tall, adorned with flowers—roses and carnations, cyclamen and geraniums, red summits on green stems; and here and there an easy chair, lamps, old English prints in greens and pinks.

One of the rooms was where my brother slept; he was always a little tired. And this was the only room where the general impression was somewhat bizarre, a re-evocation of the forthright life he had led before his death: there were banners, signal banners, from all different countries; then his cot; his dilapidated suitcase; and the black cap, with a ribbon, which had been sent back from the Island... But really I don't want to think about it, I don't want to remember...

Another small room was for me. This one was nearly empty, but everywhere frescoed with pictures of birds and cute little monkeys, blue, green, and red; the bed in the corner had the shape of a boat, and over it a sail with an island painted in the middle of it; and then a large chest that...but I really shouldn't say.... It was crammed with marionettes, dressed like real people, and I loved them to distraction. They included all my friends and superiors, as well as various authorities whom I had never met. One marionette was dressed in Chinese clothes, black and cerulean; in her hand she held a baby dragon, which was me.

The Princess wandered in, distractedly.

"What are you doing?"

"Studying."

I quickly hid a couple of marionettes, slipping them into my pockets.

"Just take a look at Anima, how well behaved he is today! His eyes so kind and ingratiating. And his nose is damp. Ah, I'm so very happy!"

The Princess' room was all pale blue, decorated on every side with large hand-painted geraniums, bright red, and with birds that seemed to sing, looking just that real. In three big airy cages hanging from the ceiling and festively decked with garlands of tea roses were twenty goldfinches: exactly the ones she had loved so much, and which Anima had devoured.

"Anima," the Princess graciously warned, pressing the mysterious cat to her throat, "you be careful now, they're not to be touched!"

"Otherwise, I'll make you pay for it," Manuele added, appearing from behind her with a small red pennant in his hand.

"Oh, son, how happy I am!" she cried, leaning her head back against that powerful shoulder as she continued, ecstatically, to hug the cat in her arms.

The sky was so calm at the villa. It was always May, and the trees were always green, the air always velvet. And parti-colored birds played at blindman's bluff, and golden groves of oranges scented the air with Eastertide delight.

Outside the park, one looked away in all directions, to all horizons, along prairies bright as emeralds, fields of grain which moved in sea-like swells; and then a turquoise strip of the sea itself, a dark and violent turquoise, almost black, surmounted by slowly billowing rose and golden clouds which crowned a delectable moon. And finally small golden cupolas, and roofs in topaz and ruby, the manifest dream of serene and stupendous cities. But we so much loved the park as never to leave it. My mother, every day, would visit the Queen, to talk about plants, cuttings, graftings, seeds… Manuele slept, or, weary, would stroll among the trees, with some one of the many songs he knew, lovely and remote, upon his lips.

"Why don't you come with me to see the Queen?" my mother sometimes asked, with an air of gentle reproof, as she prepared to go out. "Don't you think she'd find it pleasant to see you more often?"

"Who knows?!" I replied. And then, "You know how much I dislike making conversation."

The truth was quite different. First of all, I was far too much in love, far too passionately, with my docile marionettes to be able to abandon them, even for a moment. The second and more compelling reason lay in my resolute even if confused aversion, nourished throughout the years, to everything that was openly, all too openly, Good. When faced with virtuous sentiments, I was always anxious to assert my right—my clearly hostile right—to finely sharpened irony, since it seemed to me that Freedom and Intelligence grew only from the seed of an unconditional opposition to traditional sentiments. I had bought this azure corner, yet intended to keep my distance from it.

But once, my mother implored me to do her a favor. The day before, while she and the Queen had stood chatting beside the pavilion's front door, her eye had fallen upon a reddish-yellow carnation which struck to the quick of her heart. She madly desired to have it, but lacked the courage to say so to the Lady.

"See if she'll give me a cutting. I'll plant it right away..."

"Couldn't Manuele ask her?"

"Always your brother! You simply cannot do me a favor! So just go away and leave me alone!" She was nearly in tears.

"All right. I'll speak with her right now."

Resigned, I set off down the garden alley, and on reaching the pavilion, I knocked at the door. I was afraid that the Lord in person might come to open it, and, while waiting, I set to preparing an inscrutable, politely conventional face. But in fact it was the Queen who opened the door. Over a pale blue gown, for mornings, glittering with silk, she wore a short white apron. Her black hair was slightly damp and a little disorderly, but splendidly crowned by her regal silver tiara, graciously askew. One of her feet was bare, and in her hands she held a flowered cup.

"Excuse me, Ma'am, I hope I'm not disturbing you.... But my mother begged me to come. She'd like to know if you could spare her a cutting of that yellowish-red carnation. I didn't really want to come, but she'll just pine away if she doesn't have it. I see that you're busy with housework," I added awkwardly.

"Just washing a couple of cups, nothing at all to worry about," she laughed. "Children are hopeless, and no use at all. They either pilfer, or play all the time, or get into fights with each other. At that age, it's a phase they have to go through, nothing special. But come on in. Please."

"Thank you. Isn't your Son at home?"

"No, he's out in the garden looking for a little bird

that escaped last night from its cage. We'd left the door ajar...simple absentmindedness...and nobody's fault but my own."

I entered. How cool and fresh it was. Only a few pieces of white wooden furniture, brightly waxed; cages made of reeds, full of little birds which were making a true uproar. And no sooner had I crossed the threshold than they all fluttered forward to see who was there, and the liveliest one sang me a funny little poem, in my honor, amidst all the general fun. At the windows, flowers the colors of the rainbow, and cotton curtains with pink and blue circles. The chairs were caned. Sunshine was everywhere.

Accompanying the Queen, I noticed that a certain light which shone from her hovered over me as well. But it was a very gracious light, nothing sacred at all, it was something I had always seen around Anima's mistress too. In the kitchen, the Queen offered me a chair, caned again, the backrest painted with simple garlands, and with four bright green triangles painted on the seat. I suddenly remembered, quite joyously, that it had belonged to my much-loved grandmother.

"Ma'am, you know you have a really pleasant place here."

She had set to drying the cups.

"Can I be of help?"

"Don't even dream of it! In just a moment the boys will be back. And I've almost finished anyway."

A thought had entered my mind. And sitting there in that house, on that chair, watching her do her chores, I told her what it was:

"Ma'am, I thought you spent all of your time at praying."

"Me?" she smiled. "But whyever so?"

Two ruddy boys came scampering in at precisely that

moment, their blond hair flying about their heads as they chased one another. Their mouths were stained with cherries. "Give me my cherries!" one of them shouted, and the other, stuffing a handful of cherries into his mouth, shouted back, "Shove it!"

Then they saw the Lady, but too late.

Pip-pop, and two resounding slaps had reached the mouth which had uttered that nasty expression. I laughed in great surprise. The boys ran off just as quickly as they had come.

"You know, I'm really very sorry," the Lady said. "But with youngsters like that, words at times are simply useless. Are you shocked?"

"Me? Not at all!"

I was truly elated. Everything, now, was quite delightful in this house which wasn't all prayers and where people lived and amused themselves, and even where uncouth words from time to time resounded, just as in our human lives, but free from ire, and graciously.

"So much the better," the Lady exclaimed, and her smile returned to her face. "I just have to dry my hands, and I'll get you that cutting."

A few moments later she was standing at the kitchen window, searching about with her fingertips in two or three flowerpots. "I see," she announced, "that my Son is coming back. It looks as though he has found the bird."

"The one that flew away last night?"

"Yes. It's alive and hopping," she joyfully remarked. "Why don't you go out to greet him?" And she handed me the cutting.

As I left the house I ran once again into the two young boys, now huddling behind the door, whispering and plotting with their hands cupping their mouths, and with certain devilish glances in their eyes.

"Excuse me, please!" I cried.

"The little lady's in a hurry," one of them mocked, making fun of me.

"And she gives herself such airs," quipped the other one.

"I do not give myself airs...and both of you are brats," I confusedly rebutted.

Out in the garden, I found myself facing the Lord, who was holding the little bird, and a deep childlike joy washed across his face.

"Good morning, Anna."

"Good morning. I see you've found the bird."

"Luckily yes, and safe and sound, the silly little thing."

I looked at him in amazement.

"But why?... You mean there might have been some danger?"

"Well...you know...you can never tell.... The garden is quite large...."

I breathed a sigh. He didn't do miracles, and he wasn't rich or powerful; he had only his feelings and affections, his thoughts, with which to save the things he loved. Like a kind-hearted boy, just as I myself had done with Mama. No miracles at all.

"You've been over for a visit?"

"Yes. We needed a cutting from that yellowish-red carnation, which my mother didn't have."

"Did you get it?"

"It's right here, see!"

"It should grow quite nicely, but you have to be careful to water it well. Oh, you should also tell your mother that I've managed to get some samples of a new breed of roses. Maybe she'll be interested...the *Maréchal Niel*.... Remember to tell her."

"Of course. And, Sir, if you'd like to come to visit on Sunday...my brother has some really lovely books...." I gladly proposed.

He could hardly believe his ears.

"Would you like that? Of course I'll come."

The Lady was at the window.

"Mama, on Sunday we'll be going to pay them a visit," the young man said. "So there won't be any card game."

That was how I learned, enchanted, that in the evenings they played cards.

I ran off, quite happy. Manuele and the Princess were walking toward me from the villa, he quite grave and smiling, she with the cat in the crook of her arm, and inquiring quite anxiously, with gestures, whether I'd come away with the cutting.

Fantasies

It is two o'clock at night, a November night, no longer Saturday and not yet Sunday, and I sit at my table in a rented room on the top floor of an old house in the old part of the city, with the vague intention of writing a story. There is not the slightest sound, not even the squeak of a worm in the woodwork; the city is asleep, indoors and outdoors, and it's hardly cold at all. Not cold, but foggy, even if the fog isn't heavy. No more than a veil, but enough to heighten the feeling of being closed in.... But where?

I had a few ideas before sitting down at my table,but now, no sooner than I settle into my chair, they have disappeared. My ears and eyes are highly alert, to everything and nothing...because nothing is the only thing I find around me. What else could there be? And this is the one true explanation for my inability to write. My surroundings hold nothing which helps me to feel at ease, and, what's worse, even my memory knows of no such thing. To survive in this city I have given myself over to things that little by little have made me forget the others, all the others. What wouldn't I give to be able to remember them!

I drank not one but two cups of coffee, and immediately returned to my table. I switched on the light and chose a sheet of paper and slipped it into the carriage, certain that a voice would make itself heard. But nothing happened. I looked straight ahead of me at the door that leads into the other room, the smaller room where I sleep, and I wondered where that butterfly might be, the one which had slept the other night on one of the staves of the half-open shutters. A large brown butterfly with closed wings, and which actually looked as though it were sleeping. Or perhaps it was dead. I hadn't known what to do for it; whether to free it into the open or to let it into the room. I was afraid that it might feel imprisoned inside, and that outside the fog might blind it. But perhaps it was dead. All I did was to close the window, leaving it between the window and the shutters. This morning it was no longer there. Where could it have gone? If it was still alive, where could it be? And why, above all else, was it here last night, in this house, in this city?

Butterflies make you think about gardens. Once, before coming to this city, so long ago, I too was acquainted with gardens. But not so much with gardens as with the countryside, with long undulating hills dotted with groups of houses. The people who lived in one of these houses were my mother and my father and other relatives. My mother and father! They never come to mind any longer. They are buried in a village far away from here, and were buried there very long ago. But before being buried they were truly alive; they were tall and handsome people, with bright, happy eyes. All of us used to be together. I can't remember how such a thing was possible, but all of us were together. We lived in a kind of rustic castle amidst a mountainous landscape. There were many many rooms along a hallway, and finally, at the back, a terrace. You looked out into a green and peaceful valley from this terrace, and in the middle of the valley flowed a ribbon of water, a motionless stream that always sparkled of silver. At the edge of the valley, a hill began to rise, by the name of Mount Royal, a very green and simple hill, and it was there, when spring arrived, that the animal market was held. From as early as dawn, the air trembled with neighs and mooing, endless, and amorous like all the voices of animals. One heard long whinnies, or a solitary gallop at dawn. Towards the middle of the day, we too would go to the fair. It was lovely to walk between mother and father in that sea of animals and grass, to the sound of bells. It was Pentecost, or Holy Saturday; the clouds in the sky were white. Walking in the sunlight, in the fresh wind, my father whistled a few old English songs. Those were the years when all of us were always singing:

It's a long way to Tipperary,
It's a long way to go…

and he too was sorry about that. But can I confess the truth, quite honestly? All of us wondered if any such place as this Tipperary actually existed.

But this isn't what I wanted to say. Instead, I wanted to recall the way our parents talked and talked, talked continually, recounting strange tales about the countryside, and about everything that took place there. I have a very clear memory of the lamp which lit their room at night, which was also the room in which I slept. This lamp was in the shape of an upside-down tulip, but entirely white, indeed the color of milk, and with a delicate embroidery, leafy, in a tone of gray. By the light of this lamp, this dear and silent lamp, in the midst of the night, at two in the morning of a winter's night, my father, who was then a Captain in I can't be sure what army, told my mother how the country called Italy was about to undergo enormous change, at the hands of Mussolini.

I lay awake, noiseless in my bed, pretending to sleep, and I thought about this Mussolini, about the green countryside, about the lamp. What was there behind this lamp? What was going to happen, tomorrow morning?

Somewhat later—without my having learned any more about these green expanses or this Mussolini (I don't think I thought about it any more, if only for the reason that meanwhile I had fallen in love with a little boy named Gino)—we moved away from that mountain. First on a train, from which I saw the moon as it shone among the orange trees, then on a ship. Blue water was always around us, water that opened and then that closed like a fan behind the ship. My mother wore a lace hat decorated with cherries, and we were dressed in red sailors' suits. My father, the Captain, was happy.

It's a long way to Tipperary!

"Look, an island!" he said on the second day, pointing to it with his pipe. It was lovely, spotted with white houses and blue domes, blue and green.

On the fifth day, we reached a flat land edged everywhere by a smooth, white sea, and there were men and women dressed in beautiful robes, pale blue, yellow, pink, and white. We went ashore. A boy, barefoot, in a gold-colored turban came to take our bags; his face was the color of leather. We went to a windowless hotel, all white and full of a mysterious odor, an odor of lives lived out in love and savagery. The blankets on the beds were green, frayed at the edges; the lights were low. My mother took off the hat with the cherries and cried. The Captain, to calm her, brought her a plate of dates, saying, "Have a bite to eat, have something to eat."

Who knows what was wrong with my mother, because I also remember that later I would sometimes find her crying on the beach, staring out at the sea. We lived for several years in this country, all of us together, and the curious thing is that all of those years were identical. Nothing ever changed. We lived in a small white-washed house back behind the Bread Quarter. That's what it was called, since there was a square in the middle of it, a square with lots of woven mats, where merchants sold bread. The wives of the captains appeared there early each morning, beneath the blue sky, and decided on this or that enormous loaf of bread, in the shape of a sun, but brown, and all around were boys dressed in blue, with gold-colored turbans and baskets with straps: they loaded the bread-filled baskets onto their backs and carried them to the houses, walking swiftly in front of the ladies.

Behind the Bread Square was the Rug Market, a covered market where thousands of carpets were sold. To reach it one walked along a narrow little street, secluded and very elegant and decked everywhere with climbing plants; it led all the way down to the sea if you kept on walking to the end of it. Here and there, through certain low doors, one entered the Market, which was silent and at times illumined by a ray of sunlight that fired all the colors of the rugs and shone on the feet of the merchants. All the shops in the street were full of objects in ivory, in gold, in pink wood inlaid with mother-of-pearl, and leather bags, red feathers, and silver saddles. The merchants were pale-colored men, somewhat corpulent, dressed like women, with laces and veils and scarves of yellow silk. All of them wore red fezzes, cone-shaped, with a bright blue ribbon, and they didn't talk. They smoked and drank tea, smoked and waited.

From the Avenue of the Rugs, if one didn't want to go straight to the sea, one turned right into the Lane of the

Lamps, which was all a secret flurry, even in the middle of the day, with its sun and wind, of marvelous lanterns of all sizes, forms and colors. The Lane of the Lamps then led to the Governmental Palace, which was where all the captains resided, including my father. But this was a place which my brothers and I never visited, we wouldn't even have wanted to, we felt lost there.

Our lives took place, in solitude, around the house, which stood in a yellow, orderly, tranquil desert. Looking off across this desert, one could see, first of all, down in the distance, a fine, silent strip of sea, a very blue and silent strip of sea; then off in another direction one saw the oasis; then the houses where the Maltese lived, the houses of our little friends. Behind the Maltese Settlement a group of boats was pulled up in dry dock, parched and bleached by the wind and the light, and that was where we children spent the day, when we weren't in school.

I have no memory of games or voices, neither my brothers' nor our friends'; likewise I remember no faces: only that we would sit there, inside those boats, daydreaming, or perhaps even without daydreaming, barefoot and holding a piece of bread in our hands.

One day, one of the children said (to another): "Didn't you hear a gun?"

And the other: "Yes."

There was a sound of thunder, from the sea.

Then a row of white horses went by, bearing strangely dressed men, with pennants and leggings and a dreamy air, in the midst of a swarm of dark-skinned people and to the roll of drums. All the captains were up at the front, with a hand raised to their foreheads, the better to protect their eyes from the sun; their wives stood to the rear, spellbound. The sea was now flecked with long steel ships, full of flags, and sirens whistled, cannon thundered, and horses passed by like flaming clouds. It was all because of that Mussolini, who, while we were here, had occupied the country, now governed it, and little by little was spreading out everywhere.

How strange: we had thought no more about him since that winter in the mountains!

On the subject of mountains, I have to say that here there were no mountains, and not even snow. Only a torrid wind, at times, which seemed to issue from a furnace and carried a huge red cloud of dust. On Sunday mornings, in the thick of that great red cloud, a truck would stop in front of the house and we would all climb in. Ah, I think I remember the beauty of that motor's noise and of how our cries were shattered by a savage commotion; how wonderful it was with that red suffocating wind. The sky was blue on the watery horizon, and the truck sped off in pursuit of it. Blue against the soft, infinite, yellow sand. We held our hands to our hats, which the wind tried to snatch away, and we laughed. Mother and the Captain, seated up front, chatted constantly back and forth; mother too, with her delicate hand, grasped the brim of her white straw hat, its turquoise veil rippling in the air. Dear mother was no longer tearful, not in this period, excited as she was by the thought of a great plot of land which the Captain had bought at the edge of the desert. That land included a quarry, and the Captain thought to use its stones to construct a house. Our house, meant for all of us, was therefore rising at the edge of the desert, and every Sunday we went to see it. Already it had everything, except for its roof. There were ten or so rooms, already tiled in tiles containing small black and yellow stars. It had a kitchen and a large verandah beneath a portico roof held up by a row of white columns. Behind the house stood a windmill, but constructed of iron, and very tall. It pumped water from a well, of which the housing was painted green. All around, like silk, tall and smooth, shone medick grass. People say that medick grass is green. Ours was blue. I am not lying. A bright, startling blue.

We went to live in that house somewhat early, I mean before it was finished, and the happy time of our lives was suddenly over and done with. My elder brother, covered by an army blanket, lay moaning in the corner of a room. Other blankets, red or green, were nailed to the windows, because there wasn't any glass in them. In the kitchen, on the floor, a fire burned always on a hearth made of bricks, since the stove too was still missing; and all of us squatted down, in the evenings, around that fire, not daring to look each other in the eyes, since jackals howled outside. Jackals are said to be small and timid, and their gaze is said to be always charged with an air of supplication, but one mustn't cross their path in the evening. That's what made us shudder. One morning our dear little goat was no longer there: the jackals had attacked it (since she had been sick) and devoured it; we found her head in a ditch. And my brother moaned constantly and said strange things beneath his blanket. Time never passed. One would sometimes sit on the porch and watch the camel track for hours. "Today I saw an Italian...a soldier," someone would recount in the evening as we sat around the fire on the floor.

Time never passed; there was day and night, without change. Then things began to be missing. First there was Cadigia, the cow, sold to a settler. Then we also sold the horse, Stella, who was a very nervous mare with a sweet black gaze, and surely there was always something she was thinking about. Then nothing at all remained of our livestock, and we didn't even have furniture. I don't understand how it happened, but we weren't well off any longer, the way we had been before, and the Captain seemed distressed. "What are we doing here, I'd like to know?" he constantly repeated, and mother would lower her head so as not to cry. It seems that the quarry yielded no more stones, and that stones had to be bought to finish the house, and buying them meant that we had gone into debt. But the real reason, the way I saw it, if I have to tell the truth, seemed more profound: life had begun to spin more rapidly; we had to grow up.

Here we are on the sea again: and as we moved across its waters, a strange phenomenon took place: the expanse of water behind the ship grew ever more enormous, and the tract of water in front of us grew ever smaller and smaller, diminishing, becoming minute. The expanse behind us was unspeakable, and profound; in front of us the sky grew low and narrowed down like a funnel.

All of us were silent.

On the third day, we saw the Island again: it seemed to have yellowed.

The city in which we disembarked was very old, with a blue sea and its port full of red oil tankers. Our new house was likewise old, with balconies.

Here, we immediately re-entered that poverty which had started with the story of the quarry—a poverty which was also an ugliness, a chain, a limitation, and it was clear that it had to be broken. But it was part of the city itself, part of the population which increased so fearfully, and for no apparent reason. It was nauseating. So the only way of defeating it was to pack one's bags and to set out again. But how could we manage? Our parents had reached the end of their courage, that much was clear, and so the boys decided to leave. They took papers as sailors, and departed.

Now I remember the red oil tankers on which they

embarked, how they distanced into the misty dawn on the gray silent sea; how flanks and masts shone briefly in the intermittent golden light of the harbor's beacon. They leave the port, they pass beyond the jetty's black tip. Farewell, brothers, farewell.

One evening—the Captain had removed his braided cap and sat in shirt sleeves at the kitchen table—a knock came at the door: a telegram. Shortly afterwards, the house resounded with wails and laments and darkened with frightful tears; our mother, on her knees, dragged herself to the open balcony door, moaning, "my son, my son." One of our brothers had died on an island in Central America; they had buried him yesterday evening at the foot of a palm tree, and this already was the second night of the future which forever he would pass beneath that palm, under the stars of an American sky.

Stars were a part of this period. I remember how they seemed so large and tremulous in the black sky of Europe, nearly as though they too perceived that things were about to change, and not for the good. And my mother would remark, on April evenings when that winter was gone, "That's where he is. My son's up there," which didn't strike me as probable.

Meanwhile, that Mussolini of our childhood years had made an agreement with the leader of the Germans, and our country was changing day by day: it seemed every day to be more like a giant beehive, when the bees with their stings buzz menacingly through the air. They wanted to wage a war against the other part of the world, invading near-by gardens.

One of my brothers, dressed as a soldier, stood in the doorway, and my mother (I see her still) caressed his hair, saying, "God protect you, my son." "Yes, Mama," he gently replied.

From the country in which he arrived, he wrote and asked for a violin, and we sent it to him. It seems that he played it constantly, seated in a corner of the abandoned barracks, as silent as the house we had had in the desert, when the jackals wailed. But now, instead of mother, the Captain, and his brothers, he had only his violin. He played English songs, in spite of everything, including *Tipperary,* which was the tune he loved most of all. He was playing even when the foreigners came, and he didn't move, since he had no gun. He kept on playing, and they killed him. Then the foreigners buried him. Beneath an olive tree.

When the postcard arrived (this time they didn't think to telegraph) it was only a few days before Christmas, an evening full of fog. My mother's cries, this time, were weaker, and without so much as a single tear. She paced back and forth from one window to another, peering out to see if anything might be glimpsed through the fog. She hoped there had been some error, and the tiniest noise in the stairwell was enough to make her start. She folded her arms on the table and rested her head against them, and that was how she slept, repeatedly reawakening. He'd come back, she was sure of it, he wasn't asleep beneath an olive tree.

This was the period of the bombings, and when the sky was clear and one could think for a moment or so, "they came." Little by little, we had to resign ourselves to fleeing, and we returned to those mountains which had seen us children. But not to the same place. A different place, and then another. They didn't want us anywhere. We went from town to town, until finally we found lodging in the house of a family of coal miners. Here, we had truly nothing any longer at all. It snowed, the miners had flour and potatoes, and we didn't. My brother, the youngest, always slept, as though in a trance, and the Captain by now was haggard and white. This place too was one day reached by the Germans. All the men had to be shot, including my brother and the Captain, for I don't know what compelling reason. Soldiers came to wake them up and dragged them into the square and made them stand in a row. My brother was annoyed, since waking him early was always asking for trouble. They remained lined up for a good many hours—it was a fine blue morning—in front of the mothers. Our own mother was calm; to tell the truth, her face bore a smile; and when the Germans forced the column towards the woods, she cheerfully followed it. I think her mind was no longer as clear as it once had been. It was dusk when she and my brother and the Captain returned. She walked in front of them, briskly, and her eyes were as black and calm as those of the mare we had had in the desert. They shined, and shined. "Poor boys," she said, referring to the German soldiers. "A whole day without a meal, for this firing squad that then got postponed...." The boy and the Captain walked behind her, heads lowered, in silence.

And now another time. The war is over, we return to our houses and they are no longer there. Our house too has been demolished, even though its walls had only been cracked; they carried it away stone by stone, they sold it. Our city is full of people who dance and sing, and of others curled up in corners so as not to feel the bite of hunger and cold. Chaos. Nothing is certain any more. Mussolini has been shot, and then hanged. There are those who adore him, others curse him, some are discarding their uniforms, others are donning new ones. Now all the talk is about the East. The East is great and promising. A new sun will rise in the East. Everyone talks about the East, singing the praises of the East. But of the West as well. The West is rich, people dance, there's every brand of cigarettes. Which is the better place? Everywhere is better, if only there is money around. Money, money, money, that's the only thing people talk about. Grand ceremonies in the churches: funerals, marriages, and baptisms. And discussions and still more discussions in the squares. Some are in favor of one new leader, others in favor of another: but all the discussions adjourn to some colorful local restaurant. To sounds of guitars and violins.

In the midst of all this agitation, this furor, this happiness, we no longer have anything to eat. We don't have the courage to steal, so we stay off in a corner with our hunger. We've found refuge in a house, and the police arrive to throw us out, because we don't have any right to be there. So we move into another house. But this one is soon to be sold, and so we go to still another. Which is where our parents died.

My mother died in the morning, on the last day of May, with her eyes full of tears since she was sorry to abandon the garden—the gardens of the homeless were full of flowers at that time of year—and also the little cat, which was sick. She didn't care a hang about the rest of us. When her eyes closed, she suddenly turned very young—pale and young, with a sweet smile beneath her black silken eye-lashes—just as she had been when the red desert wind had snatched at her veil and the truck rolled along the road, and the African landscape beckoned to us all, saying, "Come, come...."

For a while, the Captain sat around in the garden, waiting for her to return. Then he departed as well. Nothing more was ever heard of him. Some people say they saw him a couple of times, in the evening, at dusk, motionless in the garden of the house, dressed in yellow, with a hoe in his hand...but he was pale, very pale, as though he'd been waiting for a very long time. Fantasies.

* * *

I could start all over again, if I wanted to, adding all sorts of things which here have escaped me. But all the things my eyes have seen in all these years fan fatally out into a single uniform tone, a single shade of blue, where this or that particular has no more importance than a vague eddy of foam, or a sparkle of silver reflections. The sea! That's what a life comes down to when the years begin to fill up the space between ourselves and the vaporous shore on which we first appeared: the drowsy, remote, murmuring sea.

The youngest of our brothers, the one whom the Germans marched into the woods, along with the Captain... even today I see the way he stood at my doorway, a few years back, tall and light on his feet. His black eyes sparkled like something precious, like black luminous pearls, full of courage and generosity. His forehead was smooth and calm, his voice noiseless, as though I only imagined it. His red suitcase stood on the floor beside him. He was about to depart on some ship, a ship that would reach the Pacific Ocean, and he wouldn't return for a great deal of time, a very great deal of time, perhaps not until he was old. It was night, the way it is now, already a winter night, and the electric bulb on the landing threw its light on his narrow shoulders. "You have to be patient." This is what he said to me, only this, in his calm voice which might have been a thought in my mind. "You have to be patient: then all the night will finish."

It was the last beautiful voice I heard, of that former time. And I always think back to it, even though that beauty seems now somehow illogical. "Patience!" This word would seem to presuppose a possibility, no matter how faint, a hopeful possibility that time—this time of fog and silence—can draw to an end: that this white and silent time might lose its sway. But *how* and *where* might time have an outlet? Given that there's nothing else.

I approach the balcony windows: by now nothing can be seen, or very nearly. The fog has risen to the uppermost storeys, cloaking everything, erasing all forms. The trees in the garden, green for the space of a summer, stand drowned in nothingness; the expanse of coral-colored roofs has disappeared; likewise the mountain's modest silhouette. Nothing, nothing at all. Higher up, on the right, but very high up, at the height I'd say where the moon passes by, where the moon passed in the spring, I see a red gap, like an emptied eye: the window of a skyscraper. But the building has been swallowed by the fog.

Who am I? What have I now become? What am I doing here? What am I waiting for here, closed in by a wall of fog and quiet? Clearly I am here by chance, by error; I took one train while thinking to take another, and now I am here; but I'll set out again at dawn, I'll return once again to the world of human life, where the sun rises.

The whistle of a train, then another, but very muffled. Then the noise of its cars—secret, menacing, like the noise of the sea—bites into the night. Then silence again, and the hours: three hours, four hours, five hours. And again the trains, that long dull rumble, that motionless race in the night.

God, when will all of this end! I feel a growing chill on my forehead, I am ill. I close my eyes, the illness is worse, and then something re-enters my mind: the wind of the sea and the Captain's happy voice: his voice when he was young, while he pointed at an island with his pipe....

It's a long way to Tipperary,
It's a long way to go...

Oh, but what difference does the distance make, my dears?—I reply through silent tears—just so long as our home exists, our Tipperary. Just so long as I one day see it dispel our times and fogs. With its human laughter. Our city or village. Our celestial English island.

Slanting Eyes

From earliest childhood, my love for my father was enormous. I refer of course to God, the king and absolute lord of our planet, as of all those other worlds, green with grass and water, which spin in the depths of the springtime skies.

My intelligence, no greater than a tiny bird's, already grasped the enormous measure of the gift of himself he had given me—as to all of us, by creating us. Though unable to list its wonders and perfections, my mind perceived the whole of its tenderness—since this gift, fundamentally, consists entirely of tenderness, and then still further tenderness.

I remember how at times I would stand in the open in the presence of his creatures, some huge and some quite small—the greenish sea or a likewise verdant blade of grass, a bird explosive with joy, or a flowering rose both proud and shy of its beauty. To touch or simply to observe those wonderful creatures could cause such a mountain of love to surge up suddenly within me that I feared I would die of it. I'd tremble while reaching out to touch that blade of grass, and then be surprised that it didn't scorch with love, and instead was smooth and cool. Or I'd fondle the mane of the sea with my strengthless hand; and this

Animal's muscular roar, full of unnamed pain and limitless desire, was the only thing, I'm forced to admit, which seemed to resemble the feelings that coursed through my heart.

Yet my childhood followed a fairly normal course. I learned to read and write at the level, say, of a farm boy, and I also got to be fairly good at drawing. The peculiar thing about this inclination lay in my always drawing a single face, clouded and sadly beautiful, which I naively named "my father." My mother, poor woman, would laugh whenever she chanced by one of these figures—while looking into a drawer or turning the pillows on my bed—in which she found no possible likeness to her husband.

"But that's not your father, Rachel. That's the face of a gentleman! Your father's right there, you only have to look at him."

With a tired, half-sarcastic gesture, she would point to the poor old pot-bellied man who sat resting on a chair in the courtyard, a cane between his knees, an ugly pipe in his hand.

I would blush.

"Mama, that's not my father. My father is God."

"That's what you say.... The country's King... But no such man ever married me...."

Then the good woman would shake her head indignantly.

"He didn't marry you because he's your father too. Just as he's the father of the animals and flowers, even of the flowers that aren't very pretty...the sad ones...even of the beetles...."

"All right, daughter, that will do."

At home I was taken for an idiot, owing simply to my passionate love for my true father. I thought of him always with enormous tenderness—even though never having seen him—just as the earth thinks of the spring, or as an infant thinks of the milk-rich breast of its mother.

It was only at the start of adolescence, when I was something like twelve years old, that my desire to meet my father grew truly cruel, a desire to meet and to melt into one with him, to snuff myself out in him. I was amazed that no one else sought him out, so as to clasp themselves to his knees and finally voice a long-stifled cry of love. Who might have understood me better than my father, who had begotten me with his thoughts of love? Where in this life should I go, if not to him? To remain at his side, every day to die of the sweetness of his nearness—to die from the very sight of him—that was my desire, my most urgent need.

It's commonly believed, as I too had been told, that God is an old white-bearded man who dresses entirely in green, except for a small yellow velvet shawl on his shoulders, and who stands with always outstretched arms within a frame of clouds as he ceaselessly mutters "*Fiat, fiat, fiat*...," proud and childishly excited as he sees how the things he has thought—trees, buildings, people, and animals—assume reality from the breath of his words.

I had never taken such a silly tale seriously. I myself, like very few others, knew the truth: that God cut quite a dashing figure.

While walking through the fields on springtime mornings I had seen him on several occasions, riding by on horseback. He was a fine young man about twenty-five years old, elegantly dressed, and he handled his mount with considerable flair.

He rode a thin black horse with light blue trappings, and his slender legs never relaxed their grip on the saddle, just as his agile feet never slipped from their stirrups; and his delicate hands never dropped the reins, if not to give an affectionate pat to his faithful servant.

He was earnest and calm, his neat profile sharp against the sky, and seemed immersed in dreams.

I don't know why, but I never attempted to stop him. I was too impressed, and somehow frightened, by his noble bearing.

How could he have looked at that simple little girl, with the air almost of an idiot, who hid among the grasses at the slightest sound, or who sat on the stoop of her house with her hands between her knees, thinking who knows what—that poor child who was me—how could he have seen her as his very own? Wouldn't I offend his sensibility, his love of beauty and joy? Wouldn't I be making a terrible nuisance of myself?

So there I was one morning—the sun having risen just shortly before—sitting, as I said, on the house stoop. My eyes brimmed with tears from the pain of a bee sting on a finger, and I was biting that finger between my teeth when I heard this gentleman pass.

Contrary to habit (he preferred the path through the field) he was riding right down the road in front of the house.

Absorbed in my pain, I probably wouldn't have noticed his passing, and would have lost a wonderful opportunity, if on seeing my tears he hadn't halted, and bent down from his saddle to look at me.

That was when I saw his black, slanting eyes. Their pupils were as steady as stars, and within them, though veiled, there was something as frightful as death, and as sweet as milk. As he held me in his gaze like that, motionless and calm, his lips, as soft as the earth and just that finely made, widened into a slight smile.

"Show me what you've done to yourself," he said.

I listened to his voice, which was heavy and sleepy

like the sea when it kisses the shore, or the wind when it settles to slumber among the flowers, and I began quite visibly to tremble.

There was nothing any longer for my ears to hear, nothing my eyes could see; I was lost in my Father's sweet and sinister gaze.

"Does it hurt," my Father repeated. "Why don't you say something?" he added with greater gentleness, not unmixed with surprise.

"Dear Father!" I replied.

He took me by my still innocent hand and held it for a moment in his own, which was handsome and warm, and with a strength lightened by grace.

I will never be able to describe what I felt in that instant. My throat closed up from the joy of pure abandon, and if someone had asked me, "Do you want to die?" I would instantly have replied, "Yes, please."

The sweetness I received from those sad, tender eyes, from my Father's protective, sensitive hand around my own, filled me with wonder, and with a confusion of bliss and terror.

"Dear Father!" I said again, shedding a tear.

"Had you never seen me before?" he inquired with a smile.

My Father himself was stopping for a while to chat with me.

"Not like this…so close up," I said.

"Did you think I wasn't nice?"

"But not at all…I saw these tender things around me, the things you have made, and said to myself that you must be very good."

He looked at me absentmindedly, and I felt myself shiver.

"My house and home are everywhere," he continued

after a pause. "But if you wanted every now and then to come visit me where I take my rest, I'd rather like that. I'm fairly much alone."

Having spoken these words, with a fugitive smile, he spurred his sable horse and galloped away.

At times the heart of a child is truly too small a prison for its joys, as for its pains.

I can't express what I felt in that moment, and from that moment on, for my Father, that fine young man with black, slanting eyes which spoke of so much strength and such vast, strange melancholy.

"Father, Father, my dearest Father," I called repeatedly. "How sweet," I cried. "How kind of you to discover me in this simple little beast. Oh You, who are 'I'!—Traverse me, destroy me!—Such beauty!—Beauty to be thanked for always having been, and for having allowed me to behold it! You birds, and grasses, and flowers, you supremely gracious things, may all of you be drunken with it! And please, you other horrid forms, obscure and veined with blood and soaked with pain, please forfeit not even an ounce of your hurt and humiliation, for it's from there that our Father's beatitude advances! You would roar with joy if only you could know that all of your distress is merely a necessary prelude: the night stretched prone at the feet of dawn, the blackness that lends greater light to the rising blue. May the happy exult! And may those who burn in tears and shiver in blood now smile and rejoice. For we share but a single youthful Father, and he loves us: this somber Beauty is the force of love!"

These were the effusions I shouted out, and a great deal more, until finally I was tired, though no less glad.

He had seen me, and he loved me.

I remained awake all night, sitting up in my bed as

though I had high fever, with the constant thought of his beauty and his poise which had made me cry, of his strength and melancholy which had made me shiver.

Already I was wholly outside myself, in him.

From the open window I watched the stars, shining on the black arras of the night, jewels which had issued from his hands, and I took the measure of his greatness. I saw a tree, tenderly dressed in green, as it shuddered and heaved in peace, and I recognized the gentleness of his hands, which had clothed it.

The cat that slept by the fire in its silky pelt, with its living belly and velvet paws: the cat as well spoke of my Father's supple intelligence, his harmonious sensuality and imagination.

At dawn I was still awake. All ardent and frozen in a short coat with a velvet collar, I set out for the countryside, toward my Father's house.

When I entered the garden, the sun already stood high above, and an old man was watering the plants and bushes with a green sprinkling can.

I much enjoyed the silvery rain which fell on a group of large red roses, a whole family drunkenly nodding their heads.

One rose lay on the ground. I picked it up and pressed it to my heart. In my excitement, or something else, I seemed to hear a lament.

"Rose," I asked, "what, dear flower, is the matter?"

"My Father, my Father," it murmured. "Never again will I see my Father."

Disturbed, I dropped it back to the earth.

I entered the house through a hall which was very bright and calm, and I immediately saw my Father, seated in a low chair and holding a red pipe in his hands. He awaited me with a smile.

He wore a light blue sweater, and seemed to be a little boy.

I approached him, but just a few steps before reaching him I halted, weak and childish, with no further strength in my knees. My inner beatitude, which flowed from his black eyes, exhausted me.

"How are you?" he said. "Is that finger better, Rachel?"

I held it out to him, nothing was wrong with it at all, and once again he took me by the hand.

He was smiling. My wondrous friend was smiling, my king, my youthful Father. His face! Have you ever seen how the sky and the earth peer at one another after a storm? With that ardent ambiguity, that animal peace, that strange beauty wholly suffused by a multicolored light?

The beauty and youth of the face I called my Father's brought a smile to my childish lips, a smile perhaps detected only by Heaven's radiant Angels.

"Well then… Do you simply want to look at me? But tell me, rather, about your life. How are things going, Rachel? What are your favorite games?"

I kneeled before him and rested my head on his knees. My eyes completely failed me. After a moment, I muttered:

"Father, I saw a rose."

"Yes, I have many roses," my Father casually replied. "I'm very fond of them."

"The one I saw had fallen, and was calling out your name."

"Yes?" came his gentle reply.

"Father, why did you create the roses?"

"I like them, isn't it obvious?" he said, looking at me playfully.

"You create things, but never preserve them, is that how it is?"

"No," he replied, "I've never thought about that."

He put down his pipe on a small red wood table and just barely glanced at me. Now I was crying quite freely.

"And so, Rachel?" he said, regarding me with affectionate surprise.

"Father! Father! Make is so that rose won't be dead any more!"

In his black eyes, the black slanting eyes, those calm and dangerous eyes of the youth who was my Father, I saw the passage of a flash of misgiving, an anguish, and I was afraid I might have irritated him.

"Forgive me," I said through my tears, "I didn't do it on purpose. I feel... I am so happy at being here with you.... So it hurts to think of that dying rose, which will never see you again."

Now a blush of tenderness entered my Father's eyes, a motion of pity which made those youthful eyes sublime and adorable.

"Bring me the rose that Rachel is talking about," he said to a servant who was crossing the hall, a man who was dressed in gray, and bent and tired.

The servant left the room and returned shortly afterwards, holding the flower in his wrinkled hands.

"Here it is. It is quite dead, sir," he said to my Father, and then placed it in his hands.

The flower turned fresh again, for a single instant: it lifted its tender head and *laughed* with beatitude. Then it turned livid, shrank, and crumpled together.

While bending forward to stare at the flower, with my lips and arms spread wide for the marvel of it all, I saw an indefinable light, which I wouldn't call bored, but disturbed, pass across my Father's eyes.

"You love all..." he said, "...all of my little games."

"Yes," I said, "because you yourself are inside of them."

He drew me toward him, into his arms; I smothered my puzzled and ever more piercing thoughts against his breast.

"Do you feel better now?"

"Yes, dear Father."

He dried away my tears with his handkerchief.

"Now run off, go out and play, out into the sun," he told me. "But be sure, you know, to come back, to visit me again, Rachel."

I wouldn't have wanted to leave. I had no further need of anything, other than to rest immobile on his knees and to listen to him talk; or to raise my head and gaze at the undying beauty of his boyish face.

But he had made his decision, and I had to obey.

He relit his pipe and followed me with his eyes, smiling, as I, in ecstasy, walked away.

The first moment, the first days when a creature—a blade of grass, a beetle, or a human being—meets his Father and grows familiar with him, are of mortal sweetness. It's as though we are bathed in an azure water, beyond the earth and deeper than the sky. It's as though we become the sun. We burn, and shine, and rejoice. Terribly. We would say we are nothing but light, if we didn't see that we are fire as well. A heavenly beauty takes charge, turning our husk transparent; we resemble a diamond of unparalleled splendor that burns in a wondering hand. In truth, we no longer have any such thing as a body or a human form, except for a few half-visible signs that mark our presence in the world.

When I re-entered the house, mute and ardent, those who had lent me flesh, received in turn from other beings, were stupefied; and a sad shadow—of jealousy or envy—darkened their brows. Now I no longer walked, but flew;

rather than think, I rejoiced; I didn't speak, but shone. Without observing myself in a mirror, I knew I had now become beautiful; and this knowledge contained no vanity. For in all certainty I knew my newfound light to be nothing but my youthful and splendid Father's. I was he: inside my previous girlish form I burned with love, and my gestures and gaze were strange.

Passing before my parents, I stooped to kiss their clothes, with never a word, but rather with tears of love and gratitude: for the happiness to which these arcane vehicles had conveyed me. Seated at table, I touched no food, only pretending to lift it to my mouth. I had no further need to eat, since beatitude finds nurture only in itself. Having entered my room, I stretched out on my bed and pretended to sleep. But in truth I slept not a single instant, since joy does not sleep.

Just as on the night before, I listened anew to the life of the world, animate in all its parts: the pulse of the belly of the cat; the murmur of the tree through the window; the mute and unspeakably powerful gleam of the stars. Other summers came back to life inside me, other springs; the pain and slowness of the winters. In truth I was no longer Rachel, no longer myself: I was the world. I was the blue sea of which the shores appear so veiled on pure May mornings. I was the beautiful gold-backed fishes that flash among the marvels of its depths. I was the towering snow-clad mountains that peek into view among quick March clouds. I was the wind, I was the snow, the hard rain that runs like tears and cleanses. I was the earth's seething villages: the men, their vanished fathers, their sons and daughters with flowing hair and compact flesh; their animals, and their animals' cubs, with soft, pliable pelts. I was the roses, the birds, the throats of the birds and the roses' sweet perfume. I breathed like the sea and shuddered like the wind, germinated like the earth and unfolded like the roses. I blanched and fired like the clouds. I was time, I was my Father. With parched throat, I languished with a sole desire: to lose myself in his light, so my spoils might totally burn to ashes, and only he exist. Once having seen him, how could I have hoped or wanted to remain myself? To resist his power, to close back up inside myself, to be again that small, tenebrous "I"? No such thing was *possible.* This opportunity, this fateful opportunity, could not be allowed so miserably to vanish.

The good woman who was my mother was baking bread, and the poor man in the courtyard, my father, was busy at freshening the chicken feed, and the sun shone with enchanting freshness on the white wall of the house, and on the tiny luminous flowers of the weeds along the lane, as once again I left that house to go to visit the lord who was my Father.

My hands clasped an object I wanted no one to see: a little tin knife, about two inches long, which once, before, had been my doll, and to which I still referred as "little brother." I imagined it could cut. I intended to ask my Father to take it in his hand and kill me, while never ceasing to look me in the eyes. I knew of no other way to offer him my life. I could do nothing other than to die for him, so my limitless devotion might shine in a tranquil sleep, or in a tiny splash of blood. My simple heart never doubted that he might not understand me; I was sure he would give me satisfaction. I imagined his delicate gaze, and his joy: "You want to die for me, Rachel?" A confusion of blissful words spilled across my lips, and cries of happiness swelled within my thoughts.

* * *

"Rachel, sir, is at the door."

My knees seemed hollow, my throat went dry.

"Show her in," my Father's youthful and already unforgettable voice responded to the servant.

I entered his study. My Father was seated at a table covered with papers, on which lay scattered as well a few rose petals. His hands were brightened by the papers' whiteness, and the red of the petals of the roses gave them an additional grace.

I saw his face which I so much loved to be smooth and tranquil, and his eyes tender, like those of a person who has slept extremely well.

That very same calm slipped suddenly into my heart and gave peace to all my limbs.

I felt as normal as beauty, as calm as a child in the total contentment of approaching its mother's milk-swollen breast.

He had entered me, simply by regarding me.

I approached him, ingenuously dropping my knife at his feet.

He glanced at it indifferently, as though he had glimpsed no more than a ribbon dropping from my hair, and placed an arm around my shoulder.

Its heat was a kind of benediction and robbed me of my voice.

The sun can warm you, and fire burn you: but none of that will ever resemble the heat you receive from your Father's arm. It warms your coldest thoughts, and makes them flower.

I trembled and smiled; I could do nothing else than tremble, quietly, and smile. "This," I said to myself, "is *his* heat; this peace is *his* peace."

"I was straightening out some papers," my Father remarked without releasing my shoulder, drawing it indeed more tenderly against him. "It's a great deal of work and I'm rather tired. It was nice of you, Rachel, you know, to come visit me."

"Is it work concerning the world?" I timidly inquired.

"Of course! All the sketches for the basic structures, the drawings I did in those now distant days when I still hadn't made any real decisions. The exciting thing back then was the plan itself. It's interesting now to take a new look at them, now that it has all been done."

His slanting eyes held something perplexed and tired which very much moved me.

"Father," I shakily asked, "Don't you like it any more?"

I felt his grip grow tighter.

"No, my dear, I continue to like it quite a lot."

"I do too, ever so very much." I said.

"That's only natural," he remarked.

"Because I'm very young?" I said, "Is that why you think I like it? Because I can run and play, and I have a mother, is that what you think?"

"I really couldn't say," came his hesitant reply.

"Oh, but that's not the reason at all," I continued, lowering my voice and pressing my face against his chest. "It's because of you, that's why I love this world. I sense your home to dwell right there inside it, and that's why I adore it. Everything has a meaning since you yourself are a part of it, as my friend, as a mother to me. Before I met you, I wasn't happy at all. I would sit on the stoop before the house, looking thoughtfully at the sky and the earth, and asking myself... all sorts of dark questions, dear Father! I felt like a still unfeathered bird which had fallen out of its nest. I felt that the earth was not my home, and I had no home in any paradise, not without you. My whole desire, even though I didn't know it, was directed only to you, as anxiously as the springtime sky at first light desires the loving reappearance of the sun. Nothing could appear as it truly is, as long as you weren't there."

He listened attentively, his powerful slanting eyes steadily engaging my own. In meeting that gaze, I bobbed and rejoiced like grass as it bends before the wind.

"I don't know if you often look out to survey the earth," I continued, "or if while riding your horse through the fields you observe the sadness of the things to which you do not speak, of the things you don't caress. They germinate and find renewal according to your once established plan, but with a kind of fatigue and pain, with the sadness of closed-up hearts. They pace toward the future, they cross the plains and scale the mountains of time, like armies which have lost their cherished captain. At times, Father, I listen to the sea on autumn nights, and it seems that its voice is fraught with a frightful pain—the pain of not seeing and loving you. Or when I bend down over a spider, I observe the shame with which it drags itself along on its horrid paws, wholly a creature of necessity, cruelty, and treachery, and I seem to hear a question within its minuscule thoughts. Why, it seems to ask itself...why does it have to inspire only aversion and repulsion? Ah, if only your hands might reach out and touch it, destroying its form and renewing its life into the shape of a blue butterfly. But no! Everything continues, everything renews itself, with neither meaning nor consolation, all across this earth which is dear to me. I have seen mothers crumple and fold like leaves tattered by the winter winds, after filling the mouths of their children with foaming milk; animals killed, grasses trampled, flowers cut, before their day was over. They live an almost lightless day, like ill-attired workers in dusky factories, obedient to ferocious overseers. Dear Father, why can't you turn your eyes to them? Why can't you warm them? Why don't you fill them with joy? Why do they suffer and die without having seen you, remaining untransfigured? Must they die without knowing peace?"

It seemed that the pressure of his arm around my shoulders had lessened, and that some new thought had come to divide my God from his creature.

When I dared to look up at him, I saw that he held his eyes averted.

I felt a cold, a horror.

"Father," I muttered, "forgive me."

"Do you always say such weighty things?" he asked in a low voice, and with gentle irony.

"No, no, sir. Are you very displeased, sir?"

"Yes, Rachel."

I was distraught. I could not understand. Suddenly I felt him to be very far away from me. And where was I to go, if he did not understand me? If my Father did not accept me? What had I done to offend my God?

He rose to his feet and went to stand in front of a bookcase. He was mirrored in the glass of its doors, and I could see the whole of his figure, from the front. His eyes seemed widened, and veiled, full of that "something as frightful as death" which I had seen there when I very first met him. Now, however, I felt I could make out its name: it went by the name of desperation, or of boredom. My Father was *bored*.

"You draw my attention to something I have always had reason to suspect," the young man said in a voice that was absolutely sweet and calm, but full of a gravity that made me tremble. "The episode with the rose was quite significant. I understood already yesterday, Rachel, what absurd things you demand from God."

"But what, sir?"

Those sad eyes of his, which I had adored, were no longer kind. They were no longer the eyes of my Father. Kneeling on the floor, next to the chair where he had been sitting, I looked up at him and felt that I was dying.

"Sometimes," he continued, never lifting his eyes, "one happens to construct a figure in a slightly more lively way, with lines that are somewhat more accentuated. And then that figure interrogates us, and poses questions for which we have no answers."

I took my head in my hands. My veins were empty of blood, my voice had vanished.

"You think that I am good, Rachel," he cruelly continued. "That's such a shame. I am not good. I'm just like you, and just like all the others. I am even less good than you, since you love me, and I can't do the same. Beauty is the only thing I love. I hate trials and errors, and I hate decay. Things amuse me for an hour, and then I abandon them, turning my thoughts to the search for new amusements. You mustn't think this doesn't make me sad. There's a court here inside of me: but I am the judge no less than the accused. And our evening conversations are eternal."

The servant from the day before came in, and approached to whisper something in his ear.

"I'm sorry to have to leave you, Rachel," said the youth who had been my Father, approaching me. He attempted to smile, but looked off into the distance, his air somewhat bleak.

"Come back some other time. Not tomorrow, nor indeed the day after, I have a great deal to do this week. And, if you'd like some good advice, try to have some fun, running and going out to play. Don't think so much about your Father. That leaves me rather depressed. And try to forgive me."

I got into my jacket without any help. He looked at me coldly, distantly. He saw something that shone on the ground, and bent down to pick it up.

"Look," he said, "you've forgotten this." He handed me my tiny penknife.

I left the room. My Father closed the door behind me.

Though only a few hours had passed, the weather had changed. It was dark, and raining heavily.

Oh, let me remember that great, horrid, unnatural pain which broke and wounded all the parts of my body, like a dagger wielded by my Father's hands. I limped like a hunted beast, in flight and with a trail of blood already behind it. I was nothing but shame, humiliation, and agony.

"My Father, my Father, my Father!" I repeated, "if only you knew how much I love you! Why don't you want to know? Why can't I tell you? But no, you *do not want* to know! You are tired, dear Father, and my affection frightens you. But tell me, then, where I have to turn. What am I to do with myself, if you, who are every sweetness I know, will not allow me to love you?"

I turned to talk with Joy.

"Yesterday, Joy, you were with me! Don't you remember how fine that was? And, tell me, aren't you ashamed that I remember you?"

I looked at the ground.

"Dear earth, my heavy mother—and we have no father."

I spoke to my knife.

"What are you thinking, little brother? Now you can no longer harm me! You're such a fragile thing, next to my Father's sword. See if there's somewhere on my body that bears no wound. My Father wounded me. He said to me what he had to say, and now it's done."

I looked at the sky, charged with water.

"Did our Father say the very same things to you?"

The sky wept fervent tears. The earth remained silent beneath its weight. Everything on every side was impassive pain, ancient ire, fright.

When I saw my poor parents, bent beneath the light and seated at table, I greeted them with a desolate smile, and I seemed for the very first time to comprehend that mournful weakness fixed upon their faces. It was the same sense of loss which filled my very own soul, the mournful weakness of beings that their Father has created as a game, and then forgotten.

Truly, I have never tasted a more savage pain. Stretched out on the bed which had witnessed my elation, I thought about my Father and consumed myself in inexhaustible tears. I cried until, as though totally submerged in a sea, I suffocated; and as though my tears had nearly drained away my blood as well, I was finally able to sleep.

I rested, but never forgot to turn my glance again and again toward him: glances full of gratitude for the caresses and the wounds he had lavished upon me: caresses and wounds that bore the imprint of his hands.

I awakened into a morning of untold purity. I attempted to remember what had taken place, but my mind remained blank. I rose from my bed and made my way to the window, staggering as though I had long been ill.

I saw the azure springtime sky, and once again I broke into tears, but without understanding why such beauty and calm should dash me into such a lament.

The window panes reflected the image of two widened eyes that were full of an agony of love, a melancholy joy and a tormented smile; but what cause did I have for those feelings, to what did that smile refer? I knew of nothing to which to relate them.

I no longer had any memory of what had taken place, or of *who* had addressed, enlightened, and wounded me. But something inside of me knew, and was mortally enchanted. Later I resumed my place on the house stoop. I abandoned it only to go and help my parents with their chores. Then I'd return to sit there again, in obedience to a heart which knew of something, which expected something—or someone—of which it could not speak.

Several years were to pass like this. I hadn't grown up—how can a child grow up without the love of its Father?—I was forever thirteen years old, with a thin body, a humiliated face.

People learned to disregard me, and my parents remembered my existence only from time to time.

I worked and waited—waiting to die—without ever saying anything.

And then one evening (I sat sewing before the door) I heard footsteps, and then an unspeakably dear voice speaking into my ear.

"How are you, Rachel?"

It was my young Father.

"I'm mending a handkerchief," I said.

He touched it.

"It's still wet."

His slanting eyes were more tender than milk, as dark as night.

"You know," he said, sitting down beside me, on the stoop, careless of soiling his dark suit, "after that day I did quite a bit of thinking."

I didn't dare ask, "About what, Father?" I wanted no thoughts again to shatter the gentleness of his presence.

"Don't you want to know more?"

"No, sir, no...." (I was about to say "Father," but stopped myself in time).

"You wanted to call me 'Father,'" he said with a smile.

That smile left me breathless.

"It's a shame you didn't come back, Rachel. By the following day, I was already sorry about the things I had said to you, and I wanted..."

It was just the same as the way in which rain will sometimes fall: fresh, tasteless water on a parched countryside, into the burnt throat of a rose. Inert, I drank my Father's compassion, his restorative tenderness. My eyes flushed with tears.

"What?" I asked.

"I wanted to tell you I was sad to have pained you."

"It doesn't matter, Father."

"I'm like a little boy," he added, timidly leaning against my shoulder.

I lifted a trembling hand and placed in on his head, on the forehead I loved so much. I felt him let himself go, against me, and toward me. I felt myself to be a mother, the earth. An infinite patience, a secret fidelity, a sad and tender smile, ambiguous and clear: these were the signs that defined me.

"Are you sleepy, sir?"

"No, Rachel. And you're not tired?"

"No, no, sir."

"Tell me when you are."

I smiled. He could be tired, but never again could I be tired, never, if he was tired. Now I knew that Love too is an unhappy child, and at times turns cruel without having wanted to do so. I knew—I, the Earth—because he had stopped here beside me, and had looked at me tenderly, with a tear in his slanting eyes.

The Gray Halo

The way it all began aroused no particular suspicion. It simply seemed that the season was sad.... The previous month had been quite fine, and everything had remained that way until the first or second day of May. Then the weather changed: first, a few afternoon clouds, but clouds that returned the following afternoon. Three days later it rained, not heavily, but enough to force everyone to pull on galoshes and carry umbrellas. And everyone, casting an afflicted glance around their darkened rooms, remarked:

"Looks like November has returned."

This season had often been like that, so really there was nothing new; but now—a month had passed—the return to November hadn't abated. Every now and then the sun shone through, but quickly fled; and when the sun veiled over, everyone could see—those who felt like lifting their heads—a faint gray halo around a fulgent disk. That disk was more vivid than it normally might have been, and the shadows on the ground, of people and houses, seemed darker and sharper. But the air, as though the sun had been replaced by I couldn't say what unknown star, held a touch of obscurity.

It rained for the whole month of May, and then into June as well. The colors of the flowers on the plants were sharp and vibrant, the pinks were purplish, the lilac-colored leaves of the trees an intense emerald.

There were volcanic eruptions just about everywhere, strange tides, luminous white surf on the sea. At evening, in front of our television sets, we all sat as though spellbound.

Then the newspapers started to talk in a rather unusual way—with humility, I'd say—and the same for the radio news. Some said it was an influence of Saturn. Others disputed it.

Personally, considering the life I led, in my old, slightly decrepit and neglected house, it was something that had nothing to do with me. Debts, urgent work that had to get finished, and the feeling—not very fine—of a life gone wrong. Of a world gone wrong. In short, I wasn't much worried by these new events.... I'd even say that something inside me remarked them with a certain phlegm, a not ill-disposed curiosity.

On June fifteenth, Signora Bianchi came up to see me. Her husband had been doing poorly since December, and she was worried, not for herself, she said, but for him.... Very, very distressed... From what she had read in the paper she had understood...had intuited everything. There was nothing I could say, I mean no words of comfort. I tried to smile; I offered her a glass of wine. She drank no more than a sip:

"And this talk that's going about...that they'll all be coming back? Can that be true? Do you believe that too?"

"Now, don't get excited. In cases like these one has to stay calm!"

Her eyes (large and green) were teary and tremulous, and they also held an emotion which struck me as new to her.

She moved out of our building two days later. She

had received a telegram. She took her husband and her two daughters with her. I never saw her again.

Other tenants in the building departed as well, called away by a telegram, a letter, a long-distance phone call. Others, quite to the contrary, opened their doors to new relatives...or to relatives, rather, they had long since forgotten.

I was no longer able to work. Toward the end of June my mother arrived, and on the next day my father.

As far as I remember, no special emotion, no special fuss, was attached to this return from the world of the shades. Perhaps because they didn't at all have the look of shades. They were just as I remembered them from the days of the modest life we had lived together: healthy, not particularly hardy, but healthy; not especially sprightly, but still quite vivacious and utterly themselves, and dressed in ordinary street clothes. They carried black bags, the typical bags of the poor, containing some pieces of underwear, a brush, and so forth.

I didn't ask them where they had been, since I knew it wasn't possible to talk about such things, nor did they ask me about the life I had led, or what had happened to my youth. But we embraced one another affectionately.

I gave them a room at the back of the hallway, and I was happy at night, if I chanced to wake up somewhat restlessly, with the thought that they were there. At the time, I kept a Bible in my room, and every now and then, when obsessed by a thought, that single thought which now no longer would go away, I would open it and seek a bit of comfort: perhaps we were all mistaken, perhaps things weren't so serious.

In the evening my parents would sit for a bit in front of the television set, like children, in the small half-darkened room. And I frequently observed the exchange between them of timid, allusive glances, rather as though between people who are in the know, people who share information about something hidden.... I thought I understood, and asked no questions.

Meanwhile, the events taking place all around us assumed an ever more alarming force; the populace was abreast of it all, both here and everywhere else. The enormous number of people *returning* was astonishing; even more astonishing was the tone of affection, the normal feeling of pleasure and joy, with which they were greeted. And another subtly terrifying fact accompanied these *returns*: all *departures* had ceased. The sick and the old no longer took their leave. All *departures* were suspended, had stopped. Which also explains why food began to grow so scarce. Milk, for over a month, had become impossible to find. Now bread as well. Enormous quantities of chestnuts began to appear on the market, and it was curious to eat them, boiled or roasted, just as we had done as children, in an epoch now belonging to the past.

Toward the end of July, the floods, the landslides, the eruptions had brought half the earth to a standstill; electricity remained available only in a very few areas of central Europe; England and France were in the dark, Belgium and Holland had candles. In America, an aurora borealis appeared in the middle of the day, illuminating that whole vast continent, from Canada to Virginia. In Washington, the White House was lavishly lit by torches: the assassinated president had returned, in a closed carriage which had parked throughout the night in front of the garden; Lincoln too was said to be in that carriage.

Our television set (which ran on air) gave us an image of incredible power, in spite of the lines and the way it constantly flickered. K.'s eyes were full of tears and he held a hand to cover the base of his skull, as though it still hurt him. He yelled out something, in the midst of grief, peering out at everyone with a terrible, loving, questioning expression. Then all you could see was the crowd, an immense sea of heads. Singers passed by, and lots of flags. Lincoln's carriage was decked with flowers.... But Lincoln didn't step down from it, or perhaps we didn't see that part.

Two days later, the television screen framed multitudes of North American Indians on horseback. They howled in victory. Many of them leapt from their horses and dropped in great emotion to their knees, repeatedly touching their foreheads to the soil of their much loved homeland. The cities were disappearing beneath the fury of the tides: in New York, the waters had risen to a depth of dozens and dozens of murky, white and green meters; New York City had virtually ceased to exist. On the third day, the ocean was full of wooden sailing ships, gray and decrepit like uninhabited buildings. But no, they were not uninhabited. Diaz' Spaniards, Henry's Englishmen, the Dutch, the Genovese, all of them now were returning.

The Atlantic Ocean was spewing them up in much the same way that a net throws out fish: in myriads. And they made for land where the tides had not yet reached, searching out places from which to disembark.

On the fourth day (while all of that was taking place in America) all the Czars reappeared in Russia, in full-dress uniform, the Czarinas at their sides; they mingled in the ex-royal palaces with the red guards and the aged commissars of the people.

The same sort of chaos was also taking place on all the other continents, the same upheavals in physical and historical time. People of distant epochs returned with absolute naturalness; delighted with their sudden repatriation, hordes of barbarians invaded the Moslem and

Hindu cities.... In Cairo, the pomp of the Pharaohs aroused a wave of great perplexity: the people of the lands drained by the Nile saw their ideal in Rome or London, and they took no delight in eccentricities.

But none the less, happy and contented souls were everywhere. Time had been annulled, and the mortal fear which human beings carry in their blood from infancy onward (and I believe it makes all of us greatly tremble and inwardly scream), the fear that everything passes and never returns, that life is a grandiose waterfall, the waters of which run never upstream...that fear was canceled out. That question now had received its final answer. And you noticed something funny: no one was afraid of standing judgment: a sign that humanity, basically, is profoundly guiltless.

The great monsters of former centuries returned to roam the streets of London, lean and with glowering faces, and they mixed among the kings, the queens, and the great poets. A rain of reddish mud began to fall, heavy as lead, and large parts of the populace were swathed in bandages. In Paris, the great *chansonniers* once again flourished and performed in the theaters. Mythic personalities sat in the orchestra pits: the beheaded queen, the duchesses in their crinolines, next to the women of the people and the heroines. Dumas, one day, took the town by storm: his musketeers, led by the boy from Gascoigne, crossed through the city's streets, directed toward l'Etoile: they intended to restore the government of the city to the king.

The newspapers were black with headlines; but then, before too long, papers ceased to appear. Broadsides and edicts reappeared on the walls, counseling calm and inviting the populace to trust in God.

By now the factories had been closed for all of three months. The workers spent the whole of their shifts at bars and coffee shops, endlessly arguing and talking. In the evenings, everyone went home early.

Confronted with the growing lack of air, the television station broadcast fewer programs. Everyone suffered, but there was also a very great calm.

On September twenty-ninth, the sun was encircled by two concentric halos, one green, the other black, and broken by only two or three rays of light. But such splendid rays of light.

On the thirtieth, it rose no more than a handspan above the horizon, and the whole day was nothing more than a long, enduring twilight.

On October first, every city espied the sea on its horizon. The party was over; the earth was now about to open.

A great silence followed. For two or three days it was always evening; with vast, infinite silence. The plants grew black and withered, as though in a precocious winter; the birds were silent.

Until now I have neglected to mention (perhaps because personal feelings are no longer of any importance in these kinds of circumstances) the way in which my spirits, like those of so many others I knew, had discovered a great tranquillity. I saw all of these events as a *spectacle*. I'll also admit to something more: that spectacle didn't particularly interest me. Owing to a kind of spiritual deformity, which indeed was highly common in that epoch, my soul quite largely continued to turn its interest toward all the usual, trifling things: for example, just to mention one, like paying the telephone bill, which recently had been rather high. In short, I was missing the point of it all.

Secondly, I happened to have a slight dispute with my mother. Though nothing serious, it disturbed me all the same. Ever since my childhood, she had always insisted that I shouldn't, for the love of God, use complicated hair-dos. As a girl, I had long black hair, which I had combed with a part on one side: on the right, to be precise. Now that I had given up parting my hair, and that my hair, above all, was no longer black, my mother surveyed me with a desolate eye, and then suddenly one morning (beneath that leaden, evening sky) could no longer refrain from remarking:

"Oh daughter, what have you done with your hair?"

We were in the bathroom. I stood before the mirror at the wash basin, and she was standing in the doorway. I couldn't contain myself, and without so much as turning around, I replied with sudden anger:

"Mama, please, that's all just so much foolishness! The whole universe is doomed, and you don't see it. Instead, you're going on about my hair. That's downright ridiculous."

My father heard my words from where he was sitting in the kitchen, and he advanced, all pallid, to a step behind my mother's back and peered at me over her shoulder.

"Now, Julia, dear child, what are your trying to say with all this?" he asked.

"I said exactly what I meant," I replied, but I was already sorry for having broken out.

"Well, we can't talk with you about it...we simply can't," he responded, nearly with a sob. "But this isn't a time when you ought to start insulting us...."

"I'm not insulting anyone. I'm simply calling attention to the truth."

"But not to all of it, that's what you don't see. You forget the way you were as a child, so closed and spiteful. And if you didn't want to study, what fault is that of ours?"

True enough. But, then again, what fault of it was

mine that I had been closed and spiteful. Since when do people choose their personalities? How many children have ever had a choice about their own personalities?

"Leave her alone, Giovanni," my mother at this point bleakly remarked. "There are ways, after all, in which we were at fault. We weren't always that attentive, back then, remember? We didn't understand *the enormous night* (those were her actual words) which chills the hearts of children!"

I was deeply moved, even though I didn't want to let it show. Then the intercom phone at the door began to buzz. The concierge was calling up from downstairs. To say that we should bring in the plants from the terrace, if we cared at all about them. They were burning.

While my father returned to the kitchen to finish his meager cup of coffee, I went out onto the terrace, followed by my mother. But I found no trace of any kind of fire, and indeed, in that particular moment, I had the feeling of a huge ruse, nearly a delusion of the senses, of which the whole world was the victim. The air was charged with a grayish light, but a tender light, not at all spectral. The light of Easter week. And all three of my oleanders, as well as the wisteria, were fresh and green.

"Look, they've revived, thank God," my mother said, going up beside the wisteria and touching its petals.

In that moment, I saw her as though in an old snapshot, unassuming, gray, and yet with a smile so clear, sweet and youthful. I watched her. She didn't look up at me.

"Mama, you're not angry?" I said.

"How could I be?" she quietly responded.

"My hair is no longer beautiful, but yours is, Mama." I said with a tremor in my voice. "How would you explain that?"

"There's nothing I can tell you, Julia; but don't be sad. And you mustn't," she added after a moment of uncertainty, "pay back evil with evil...."

"I won't...I'll try not to do that Mama, I promise."

The world was to end at dawn on the following morning; that, at least, was what everyone said. On the previous evening, there was a great hurly-burly of people scurrying about: apartment house neighbors exchanging apologies for not having spoken to one another for years and years; maids in tears as they returned a stolen handkerchief; children phoning to uncles and aunts and grandparents; friends making up with one another.

Night had descended on the city: the world's last night.

The cathedral—I could see it from the window—shone with its thousands of white spires.

My mother, who had never been given to idleness, returned to some of her needlework.

My father sat leafing through old magazines.

I myself spent the night in my room, writing, in a whirlwind, letter after letter: to the telephone company, first of all, and then to friends and to institutions which on various occasions had given me a helping hand. I apologized. I noted the amounts, to show that I hadn't forgotten a single penny, I did all the sums. I turned my thoughts to nothing else.

The first hint of dawn appeared in the narrow opening of my window: a brightening shadow, rather than dark, still distant light. And not a sound, no single noise, could be heard.

"That's it.... Here we are!" I thought.

Rising at dawn and rushing to the kitchen to make a pot of coffee has always been one of my greatest pleasures.

I hurried that morning as well. I dashed off a cup right away and then prepared two more on a tray for my aged, beloved parents. I was content with myself, especially after that letter to the telephone company. My conscience was at ease.

I went to the end of the hallway and knocked at the door. No reply.

I pushed it open: in the pale morning light the two beds were made, the room in order, but there was no trace of my dear Maria and Giovanni.

I was about to rush to the terrace (I knew how much they had loved, when they had been alive, to water the plants on first waking up) but suddenly I had the feeling that I wouldn't find them there. They were gone. Their imitation leather bags, and their poor belongings, had all disappeared.

The tray dropped from my hands. I ran out into the corridor.

The front door was open, and I glimpsed them just for a moment—their meager shoulders, the pure white hair on their heads.

"Mama! Papa! Oh, don't leave! Come back! Don't leave me here, in this inferno!" I cried.

But they didn't so much as turn around, and a moment later they had disappeared.

I snatched up the intercom: a sleepy voice responded. They hadn't seen them—they were still asleep down there—whatever was I talking about?

So I closed the door behind me and went trembling toward the kitchen, where I opened the window.

My thoughts no longer had anything to do with the end of the world, nor with any of the events which had taken place. I could only think, with terrible fervor, of the hours in which they had been near to me, with their gentle goodness, their loving fidelity, and I had not understood them.

I cried and cried.

Then day arrived, a day like all the others, as always, when the earth had been in no danger, and I understood that now again the earth was unthreatened.

There remained only a sense of enormous distance between human beings and their roots. A sense of the loss of the dead, from the English poets to the assassinated presidents, to all the people whom people have loved and continue to love.

Which for me included my mother and my father.

My tears were full of unspeakable joy, since I had managed to call them back; and full of mortal sadness, since I had called them back only in dream. I went sobbing out onto the terrace. In the fresh daytime air, I listened again to the dark, usual hum, the dull hum of life which was starting up again.

Nothing had happened, everything was fine, life was going on, was continuing....

And now I am here in the evening, a tranquil evening, and I look at the bush of wisteria that my mother touched with her fingertips. Its flowers make a coat of smooth, pale purple. A bunch of them, the highest, is lost in the black tranquillity of the May sky.

It is a precious evening: green and black, and in the black there is pink, in the green, turquoise.

A radio, behind the wall, quietly broadcasts the usual news. I remain there with my eyes wide open. I faintly smile.

A Night at the Station

The Chief Inspector received us in his office in the building's left wing, just a few steps back from the vast terminal platform at the head of the tracks, and directly in front of the yard's last siding. One of the many doors that opened onto this platform led into a ill-lit corridor where an usher sat at a table and was reading a newspaper. He seemed to us, in the insufficient light, to be far too tall and lean and not in good health. From the moment we had passed through the doors of the great entrance hall downstairs, we had felt an unease, a reluctance, and even perhaps a mild revulsion for every feature, every detail, of the whole enormous railway station. It was a feeling for which we couldn't have named the cause. The febrile flow of humanity harbored a kind of immobility; those solemn walls a touch of oppressive lifelessness, which made them seem even loftier. The dark rain outside coalesced with the scant light in the building's interior—or surely with a light too feeble to impugn the weight of the high, black vaults; of the broad, black, cast-iron roofings; of the columns, panels and teeming decorations in Assyro-Babylonian style—and together they aroused the same discomfort that plagues a visit to a place long uninhabited, yet still charged with the breath of unknown persons who once had filled it with life.

The Inspector, at the table in his office—the second door down the corridor we had entered—offered a greeting which at first was edged with a certain perplexity. Then, after hearing the reasons for our visit, he smiled and, indeed, made no attempt to hide a benevolent curiosity. He was elderly, but small and agile, with a face the color of wood, marked by a web of minute creases, and with eyes just a touch more bright and intense than usually encountered. He was conservatively dressed in a dark suit and conveyed the impression of an aging naval officer who had spent some thirty years at sea and now was assigned to a port authority. We wanted to ask a few questions about how things work at Milan's Central Station: the movements of rolling stock and passengers, general facilities, possible organizational problems, the number of local employees, and finally a bit of information on overall costs and returns. We wanted to have an idea of the commitments and revenues that center on this sort of organism, which counts as one of a modern industrial city's most vital and complex fixtures. We saw this as our starting point for a fairly technical article.

Either he hadn't quite understood (for a moment or two he seemed somewhat distracted, rummaging about in a drawer while listening to what we had to say), or we hadn't posed our questions in quite the best way. And now he felt reluctant to call attention to the error in our approach. In either case, he offered no replies to our queries. He had taken a folder of papers from a cabinet, and he laid it on the table with a certain misgiving, a timidity that didn't correspond to the stiffness and distance of a true bureaucrat. Out of that folder came two or three largish photos of the network of tracks and loading platforms as seen towards the north, from cabins A and C; a couple of narrow-format technical journals, with green covers; and finally a color snapshot of the Inspector himself, standing dark against a turquoise background: that same thin, sallow face, surmounted by a visored cap, angled up on his forehead. He smiled almost warily, a slight grin at the corners of his mouth. "Here again, I didn't come out very well," he modestly explained. His voice was dry and somehow fragile. "You see a lot of wrinkles."

That wasn't really true. Wrinkles were displayed instead by the city. That part of Milan, those five black roofing sheds, that hill of five black semi-circles, forming what looked like the body of a spider which had dropped to the earth on tense and extended legs; that flooring, that vast roadbed covered by a dense, intricate web of railway tracks, of upright poles and steel boxes; those immobile railway carriages like strips of shadow; those vague wisps of smoke rising here and there against an horizon of stone; those working-class houses glimpsed in the distance, of exact, joyless stone: all of it formed a face, the lineaments of a scowling, hard, strangely aged and hopeless face.

We had nothing before us but a handful of photographs, yet already that initial sense of misgiving had turned into a pained, secret terror, of much the same sort that makes prisoners cast devouring glances at the walls that lock them in, forever in search of an opening. We felt the Central Station to lie on top of us like a mountain: its potency was a limit and a confine: this was a place of no departure: one entered it, and all further destination remained unknown.

Seeing us to be so absurdly attentive, so clearly immersed in thoughts that lay outside all normal channels of interest, the Inspector suddenly returned, with a touch of pique, to what must have been his customary attitude:

an attitude of fatigued authority, and of cold and somewhat disappointed expectation. Ever so slightly drumming a finger on the surface of his desk, he remarked, with incipient sarcasm, "...And I'll offer you a bit of advice. Subjects like these require a certain amount of expertise, of specialized knowledge.... Otherwise you run the risk of getting things all wrong, just by slipping up on a figure.... But perhaps you're aiming mainly for local color...."

"That too," we replied confusedly.

Adding no more, he let us find our way to the door.

Back outside, crossing beyond the main platform and into the concourse behind it, we discovered that a change had taken place inside us. We looked about embarrassed, the photographer and I, attempting to sense a volume, a note of humanity, any substantial scale at all in which we might have been reflected. But no such reassurance was possible. We felt like a couple of insects, and such obscure insects! With a life-span of only a single day, with neither memory nor hope, impassive.

The place was just that vast and dark.

During the day, and at night as well, this air of immensity and darkness is something that the hasty passenger fails to notice. But for a person who has come through the center of the city with goals like our own in mind, crossing through streets and squares electrified by lunatic traffic and awash with crowds that seem in their speed and gravity to pursue the most sublime of purposes, which instead are less than futile... for a person who issues from those straight, frozen winter streets, or from streets parched by the summer sun, and thus from out of that forest of living stone which is Italy's capital of productive labor, for the single purpose of entering this place so as to get to know it better... such a person on piercing its flanks has no real way to avoid taking notice, thanks precisely to the contrast, of these features which are worthy of an ancient cathedral: immensity and darkness. One also feels these features—though surely the impression must be wrong—to spring from the whole of this capital of labor, which suddenly seems, in spite of its benign and cordial face, to consist entirely of immensity and darkness.

For the last two days we had been making notes on all the details of this mammoth construction. It is truly imposing, and no real picture of all the activities that take place within it, like no full expression of all the pain and the range of thoughts which in fact it excites, is in any way possible, if not by way of a brief account of all its exact dimensions, with a hint as well on its general lines, and on the types of stone and marble which were used to raise it.

It was begun on April 19, 1906, and completed in 1931. Stacchini was the architect commissioned to plan it, and it occupies a rectangular area of four hundred and twenty thousand square meters, extending to the south and north between Via Sammartini and Via Aporti for a distance of two thousand meters, starting from Piazzale Duca d'Aosta and concluding at the confluence of the Rho-Monza and Bologna-Genoa trunk lines. Of these four hundred and twenty thousand square meters, sixty-six thousand five hundred are covered by vaulted roofs, of a length of three hundred and forty-one meters. The central roof reaches a height of thirty-four meters and ten centimeters, flanked by lateral pairs that rise to twenty-two meters and thirty-two centimeters, and to eleven meters. The rest of the area is occupied by the road bed of railway tracks and by the building for passenger transit. The pairs of track beneath the roofing number twenty-four, whereas the total number of rail lines is eighty-one, for an over-all length of seventeen thousand two hundred and two meters.

The road bed and a large part of the building for passenger transit lie at a height of seven meters and forty centimeters above the level of the surrounding streets and constitute the so-called "railroad level."

Seven ACE cabins contain a total of one thousand one hundred and forty levers that activate switches and signal lights.

The purely technical layout—the railway system true and proper, the tracks, the cabins, the service facilities—couldn't be called exceptional other than for its size; and its notable extent surely accords with the needs and geographical locus of a city like Milan. But with respect to the structure that houses it all—the spaces, the volumes, the whole architectural framework of the building for passenger transit—one has admit to finding oneself in the presence of the absolutely unusual.

The facade: there is simply no way to conceive of this facade if not by juxtaposing a series of slightly faded images from geography and history books: various views of distant monuments and the world's most keen and savage solitudes. Here an Indian temple, there an Aztec ossuary, and then some Egyptian tomb and a sad, white, Roman pallor. More than forty-two meters tall and a hundred and eighty-five meters long, inclusive of various receding parts, and sheeted all over with masoned Nabresina stone, it forms a kind of mountain of useless horrors, an altar of decadence, a beacon of blindness. One observes it and has the impression of touching the very pulse of modern life, the pulse of the human individual sucked up into the vortex of industrial civilization, which later, some thirty years later or so, will hand back a robot or a scrap of junk.

Three wide portals, enormously wide, each flanked

by a double pair of columns, stand along the edge of an atrium that boldly juts forward from the center of the monument. Eighteen secondary doors, surmounted by eighteen towering windows, their glazing shielded by iron bars, punctuate the wall at the atrium's rear, to the right and left of the portals, and heighten the facade's disquieting air. Above and behind the three portals, there rises another construction, again halfway between Egyptian temple and railway depot, and here the windows are nine, apparently of smaller dimensions, likewise covered by grates.

Still higher and receding farther back than this second architectural structure, there swells a third, which from the side has the aspect of a church; it shows no openings of any kind and is blazoned instead by a frieze of bas-reliefs. Again it's surmounted by the same dark dome. And now one might imagine that the series of buildings had come to an end. But many meters lower than the third and tallest, another appears to their rear: equally abstract, covered again with bas-reliefs, and crowned again by its roof. Finally, running parallel to the rows of track that issue from the rear of this building, come two lateral wings, each of a width of thirteen meters and a length of one hundred and fifty; and the area between these flanks is the space which is overtowered by the giant humps of the five vaulted roofings that offer protection to the sidings, the wagons, and the crowds of passengers as they mount and descend from their trains.

So much then for its outer appearance. Perhaps it is only lurid and a study in horrid taste, and nothing more; and if we limit ourselves to regarding its outside walls, to considering only the shell of this declaration of aesthetic rights on the part of the turn of the century, its meaning would hardly be likely to exit the field of reflections on the useless. But enter this monument! Discover its vitality! Observe its flow of humanity, in black, scampering rivulets! Attempt to detect a relation, any relation at all, between the rhetoric, the classical posturing, the funerary fullness of this architectural system and the human beings, the crowd no less distracted than remarkably intent of anonymous Italians who traverse it every day and you discover this polished dementia to have passed beyond the bounds of artistic fakery. It was also a manifesto. And it was not the bygone century that closed its doors with such a declaration, but the new one that opened them. The black pennants of the forest here flutter again over the heads of human beings; endless lines of spent and anxious men and women here ceaselessly file toward goals that only a few might call the highest good: toward the raising of works which day by day absorb the efforts of ever more men and women, and which with ever more exact and calibrated methods at last strip common humanity even of its final vestiges of energy, bringing lives that were voted to always more urgent and rapid gestures, repeated millions of times, to the total ruin of all personality. The dismal lies that swear to the unencumbered future now open to the human individual, on work as the universal ladder toward equal rights and common gain, here reveal their unintelligent fixity. Look at these heaps of stone, these walls as tall as mountains, these vaults as lofty as clouds, this iron, this smoke, these lamps; listen to the tedium that issues from the megaphones, ordering the crowd to circulate in this or that direction; observe the forward snap of the hands of the clocks, of the two hundred clocks that everywhere hang in this muted light; turn your eyes to the queues that stretch before the ticket counters, to the worn-out shoes, the shabby luggage; proceed to the trains and look through the windows at the profiles lolling back on the necks of the old, at those thrust forward by the not yet old and the young, by all the not yet old and all the young, no matter their social condition. Their anxiety, the motionless stare, the pressed lips, that stunned interior immobility of someone who imagines to be running, while instead being dragged by an outside force which alone is the thing which is running, with loping pace and yet without noise or sounds of breath that might betray its presence—their anxiety will give you for a moment an exact perception of the nature of the times we live in: the progressive contraction of personality; automatism; the death of the word. Great and monstrous idols which have issued from the minds of men have filled the skies and covered the grassy horizons. Construction is everywhere feverish, cathedrals are raised to novel gods: the dominion of profit, productivity, and apparent happiness; and lain to rest beneath them, the memory and goodness of the human being.

The photographer who had come along with me was a fine young man from this part of the world, and he displayed that modest and earnest air, that open, almost childlike face of the peoples of the North, over whom life seems to slither like rain on a pane of glass, leaving no traces. But while casting a fleeting glance at that generous face—which too was remarkably intent as it peered toward the heights and all around, perhaps searching for a first point of view from which the camera might relate to our surroundings—I seemed to note that the eyes had grown suddenly deeper, and I read that gaze to hold a sadness, the dismay of a person who after a lengthy absence had come back home and could no longer recognize the street, the dooryard, the windows of his house, nor rediscover the greetings of familiar faces: the dismay of a person who has suddenly understood that everything has changed, that all the people with whom some love had once been shared are dead, that the house is now in the hands of others who have utterly overhauled it.

"Where's Milan?" That was the question those Lombard eyes appeared to me to ask. And this, I imagine, was the very first time that the man had happened to ask it. He had been born in this city, and here he had lived and worked for more than thirty years; and nothing had struck him as too much to bear for as long as he remembered that he lived in Milan. But now, as though after a bend in a traveler's road, the city was no longer there. Or, better, its fine, honest face had assumed an expression of savagery, which had totally undone and canceled out its dear, familiar features. This monstrosity of stone, of iron, of smoke, which twenty-four years before had symbolized the hopes and greatness of the Lombard capital, today—like a powerful chemical reagent—brought to light only its human decadence, its sadness, its hollow gods. But frankly to face this fact was quite impossible for a person who wanted to stay alive. And the photographer had to stay alive.

"I think we ought to start with the concourse, the upstairs gallery," he said to me. "We'll get some good material if we come back tonight at around eight o'clock."

"Why at around eight o'clock?"

"Important trains will be leaving, or arriving. We'll find the right kind of movement. Stations," he explained, "are a bit like churches. Once the main services are over, in the morning and the evening, they're damp and gloomy. They get that sweet, blasted smell of tombs, the same uncertain lights. Things always have to be seen at the moment when they show you what they're all about."

"And not at others?"

"At others they don't exist," he said.

* * *

When we next set foot on the concourse, all of the station's two hundred clocks would in fact be pointing to "eight o'clock."

Outside, it was no longer raining; the gray, overcast day had released all its water, and the air had a certain sparkle, but it was cold.

We decided to buy tickets for Monza. These scraps of cardboard, exhibited on demand, would give us the right to remain in the station throughout the night, and to enter the third class waiting room.

While the photographer leaned forward at one of the ticket counters and spoke to the salesman, I tried not to see too much or to look at too many things. Yet even so, through my half-closed eyes, the station continued to intimidate me: the hall's inhuman scale; its ceiling where the air disappeared into a great high vault, like a sky of stone. I closed my eyes entirely, but the image remained. The building's walls, sheathed with travertine marble, descended like the flanks of mountains, closing up the place into its solitude, and along those terrible surfaces there now appeared a series of statues, like sentinels in stone: effigies of Science, Agriculture, Commerce, War, Peace. There were also bas-reliefs: showing Rome's Foundation and Apotheosis, the triumph of Caesar, the landing of Aeneas on Italy's shores. Surely they were far from beautiful statues. Indeed, they did not seem to be statues at all, but gigantic encrustations of smoke and fog. Dim electric light bulbs glowed at their feet.

During the last few moments, while the photographer tarried to talk at the ticket counter, I noticed a shadow—hardly more conspicuous than the shadow of a child—as it roamed indecisively about the hall. This diminutive figure then finally revealed itself to belong to a man of indeterminate age, frail and weightless in his well-worn suit. His large black eyes held something for which I was never to forget him: a sense of memory and as well of anxiety so absolute—and forming the ground of so fine a desperation, a death so utterly polite—as to cast a glow that flushed right up to the roots of his hair. That hair lay gray on his clouded forehead; his face was likewise gray, in addition to round, and resembled the snout of a cat. His eyes shone with a sweet, wry light, very ill. His clothes were unkempt and he paced back and forth, apparently at grips with disturbing thoughts.

As the photographer turned in my direction—the queue before the counter moved forward a step or two—this passenger (as I naturally believed him to be) approached us:

"Excuse me, doesn't the Paris express come through at nine o'clock?" he asked in a thin, high voice, and with a nearly ceremonious nod of his largish head. His smile, moreover, always remained the same.

"At nine-thirty," replied the photographer.

"But doesn't it come from Verona?"

"From Venice. It stops in Verona at seven-thirty."

"I'm sorry to have bothered you for such a little thing, but I can't make it out. I imagine they must have changed the schedule. The last time, we passed through Verona just a few minutes after seven."

"The last time?..." said the photographer.

"Yes, the last time."

The photographer kindly inquired, while better arranging the flash in his shoulder bag, and just to have something to say:

"Are you expecting someone?"

"A relative."

From the way he had said it, you could tell he had made up his answer on the spot.

"And does it take very long from here to Paris?"

"Nine hours," the photographer replied.

"A fine city, isn't it?"

The photographer didn't respond.

Shortly afterward, we left that citizen behind us and mounted to our destination at the top of the long flight of steps.

The photographer had been quite right: this seemed to be the busiest hour. The ship-like hall emerged, at least at that moment, from an agitated sea of heads, arms and shoulders. Yet all this animation seemed most likely to have little to do with the arrival or departure of this or that important train, and instead was due to chance, to that mysterious brew of interests that often brings people together in a place for the most disparate reasons, or for no reason at all. We knew that this great hall, like the vast café and restaurant at its further end, was at many hours of the day, and especially at night, a gathering place for citizens who can't make up their minds to return home, or who have no homes to return to. Among the crowd of departing or arriving voyagers, these aimless persons could be recognized by their lack of haste, and by their decorous, unassuming attitude. Unruffled people, people who have no ear for the whistle of a train, and for whom that whistle leaves memory undisturbed. Clasped hands, bodies strolling back and forth, idle conversations. And everywhere around them, a stream, two streams, of humanity: two streams which issued from the exit on the right and grew suddenly larger, swelling, expanding, and then splitting into any number of rivulets that crashed into the hall and gorged it. The enormous, opaque globes hanging in bunches from the ceiling or held up here and there on posts, cast a milky light which expanded in every direction, sometimes striped by red or green from this or that neon advertisement, and the rapid faces in the crowd flashed first one color and then the other. Voices, agitated cries for attention, exclamations from friends who had made out someone in the crowd. The 8:18 express from Bologna had arrived, several minutes late, and its crowd of passengers mingled with another from the train which came from Chiasso and beyond, all the way back to Hamburg and Stockholm. The crowd of exiting passengers stalled and parted for lines of entering passengers who struggled forward against them: trains were departing for Venice and Bologna, and there were travelers who after reaching Venice would continue on to Trieste, Vienna or Prague. Or from Bologna to Florence, Rome and Naples. And by boat from Naples, as from Genoa, to sunnier, more distant lands.

Such distances, fatigue, and anxiety, and as well a silence that every passenger carried within, could all be felt in that living wave which swelled toward the exits and invaded the descending stairs, or which rose up along them from the other direction and headed toward the entrance gates to the railroad level and the tracks.

Slowly, almost without being aware of it, we moved toward the left wing of the main concourse. Here, the restaurant and café, dimly lit—the modern cafeteria seen there today had not yet been opened—enticed us into their high-ceilinged rooms, with slightly dusky mirrors for decorations. Here the light was less dazzling; indeed there was little light at all, and silence.

As we were about to enter, we cast a glance at the outside tables.

A small group immediately attracted our attention.

It was a modest family, clearly from the south, bivouacked behind a table, off in a corner. The striking thing, on looking at them, was their silence: the silence and absolute immobility in which they were immersed.

The mother (she was doubtless the mother), tall, scrawny, and serious, wearing an open, black, knee-length coat over a summer dress with green polka dots, sat with her hands folded in her lap, beside her a swollen, misshapen suitcase. The father, who was likewise sallow, thin, and pinched, and with some sort of pimple to the side of his sharply curving nose, seemed worried, though perhaps was merely sleepy. Then there was an old woman, a girl, and a boy maybe seven years old. Only the girl and the old woman, each in her own way, showed a touch of charm, the girl with a red ribbon around her hair, and the old woman, all white, in a dress with pale blue flowers. The boy was ugly, and scowled behind his glasses. All around the family were carrying-bags, satchels, suitcases, and even a make-shift cage that appeared to contain an animal—perhaps a pigeon or a hen. On the table stood the remains of a boxed lunch, an omelet or some cheese, consumed with a sad jug of milky coffee.

The photographer, rapidly taking hold of his camera, looked at them; but the mother of the family turned around as he was stepping back to get a better shot. Having seen his maneuver, she quickly lowered her head and covered the face of the boy with her free hand; only two eyes, behind two circles of glass which had slipped to one side, peeped out above it.

The photographer attempted to laugh.

"Sorry!" he said, embarrassed.

The family, except for the mother, who had bent her hard and hostile face to her knees, now looked at us with interest.

"Journalists?" asked the father.

"Just trying to make a living," the photographer replied.

"My wife," the man addressed us with a heartfelt gaze, full of shame, as though begging our pardon, "still hasn't made peace with this world. She sees everybody as an enemy, even the best of people."

The accent made it abundantly clear that they came from the south, but one couldn't tell from quite what region, though probably Puglia or Calabria.

"You have a train to catch?" the photographer asked, after a moment or two.

"I'm afraid we do."

"The bride is dead, and life is over," came the old woman's ditty in a dialect quite close to Calabrian.

"You didn't like it in Milan?"

"Sure I liked it, but what does that mean? The work we do isn't much in demand these days; the industries are very big. I'm a tailor, sir, and sick to boot: the climate. My wife does nothing but cry. She cries day and night, and never shuts her eyes, the house is dark, the sheets hung out in the courtyard never dry, they all turn green, just the same as we do. So I say, let's go back."

"The cock crowed and told the sun to rise, the sun said, 'shame on you.'" Another snatch of song from the old woman. She seemed totally somewhere else.

The tailor's face had shriveled up, and grown miserable. He looked at us as though expecting words of deprecation, like boys at school, if their families are poor and they haven't come prepared with the things that teacher told them to bring. He seemed to feel the weight of an unlived life.

"So here we are, right where you see us," he concluded bitterly.

The boy, who until then had only listened, now spoke up to ask, with the cracked, shrill voice of a gramophone:

"Pa, but when are we leaving?"

"Right away, son."

"And we're going to Milan?"

"We've already been there."

The tailor turned in our direction, smiling:

"He always says the same thing. Because we got here at night, and he never left the house. I never saw it very well either: they say it's big, and full of lights. Is that true?" he asked, with curiosity.

"Well...yes," replied the photographer.

We said good-bye and were about to walk away when the boy's voice, hoarse and grating, returned:

"But we'll never go to Milan, never."

"We're going now," said his sister, concealing her laughter.

"On the train?"

"On a golden train. And there are gardens on it, and the sea. And the King says, 'Luigino, this palace belongs to you. Starting right now, all you have to do is give orders.' And they dress you up in velvet. And then they put you in a coffin."

"No!" cried Luigino.

"That's how it is in Milan," his sister said, "first they do this for you, then they say that to you, and then you're dead. Isn't that right, Pa?"

"How should I know?" said the tailor, gloomily.

Luigino cried.

For a moment that slow crying—the crying of children who have difficulty breathing—the grandmother's song, and the sister's laughter grew confused with one another, and then were dispersed by other voices, other noises. And the waiters kept passing by, repeating at every moment: "Can I help you? Would you like to order something else? Have you been waited on?" And the whistle of a train, remote while yet very near, painful and affectionate.

"Track seven... Track eight... Track nine..."

"Now arriving... Now departing..."

The utterly black sky, the riveted iron sky of the roofing sheds, every now and then appeared and disappeared above a thousand signal lights, as though it were obscured by billows of smoke; whenever it emerged, it was soon to be swallowed up again.

The platform beside the Paris express had quite a different atmosphere.

It was not a marvelous train, but surely comfortable, and with many sleeping cars. For anyone viewing it from the outside, it had the air of a pleasantly furnished, well-lighted house, slightly secretive, and quiet and happy. Many of those heads leaning back against velvet cushions were blond and nonchalant; many of those hands held a cigarette, or a glass, or a book, and were delicate and smooth. Here again there was silence, but a silence laden with bounty, with the odors of cloth, leather, and cologne. On the landing at the side of the train, men with black, animal faces and white, sparkling eyes moved back and forth between the railway cars, checking levers and wheels, cleaning the windows of the carriages, rapid, silent, and intent.

"Step along, please."

The cat-faced man who in the hall in front of the ticket counters had asked us earlier for news about the train from Verona was also on this platform, as lost and weightless as a little beast.

"I mean you," cried one of the platform guards. "Are you boarding this train?"

"No, I'm only waiting."

"So step aside!"

The train moved, but didn't yet depart. The windows lurched forwards and then again backwards, and this citizen's large, feverish eyes, the hungry eyes of a child, bright and mute, fixed themselves on their surfaces.

The photographer addressed him, while adjusting the settings of his camera:

"You can't say they've got the best of manners."

Silence.

"Or an easy life, either."

Silence.

"Weren't you waiting for a relative?"

"Yes.... No.... I mean, yes; I haven't been able to spot him."

A newspaper vendor, standing beside his cart just a step or two away from us, leaned toward the photographer's ear.

"The gentleman," he said with a shade of disgust, "waits for a relative every evening."

The Lombard photographer's face gave no legible sign of anything.

"There, that's done." He had taken a number of photographs. "But hadn't he sent you a telegram?"

Again, the cat-man didn't reply. He seemed to be paying attention to something we could not see, just over there, on the train.

"No, he didn't send a telegram. But I know he's coming."

"And meanwhile, you're out for your walk," said the photographer, with a smile.

The man responded with a indecipherable mutter.

"Not a very pleasant walk, most likely. This station is no great meadow."

"There's a great deal of smoke," the little man remarked.

"Smoke and iron."

"The lamps are lit, but they don't give much light, have you noticed?"

"They give barely any light at all."

"I don't dislike it. But when I came here as a boy things were a little different."

"Different, how? Excuse me, I haven't introduced myself," said the photographer.

With a certain hesitation, like a child with something to hide, the man pulled his hand from his pocket, a fine neglected hand, pale and sensitive, which visibly trembled.

"I haven't introduced myself either." He said his name. And then, "Professor of letters. I'm honored."

"Letters? Here in Milan? At a lyceum?"

"No sir. A tutor, privately employed."

"All aboard. All aboard," began a call still in the distance.

Enchanted, sparkling, and full of pained excitement, the professor's eyes returned to perusing the tracks.

"Trains are constantly arriving. And several, I think, are due in back and forth from Switzerland. That's another of the routes for France, I imagine," remarked the photographer.

"Yes, that's another."

The express departed. It slipped away like a ship, full of lights and precious objects, of comfort, well-being, and mystery. Those passengers were like gods, high above all prisons of necessity or poverty. In its place stood an empty blackness, a white smoke, the rectilinear desert of the railroad tracks. And the professor who stood on the platform and looked at those tracks with a weak, desperate gaze.

"So, you teach in Milan," the photographer now continued quietly, adjusting the way his cameras hung about his neck. He spoke with an air of indifference, absentmindedly. "Since before the war, probably. And, tell me, how was it, how was it back then?"

No reply.

We walked for a few minutes, one beside the other, in silence, directed toward the main platform, toward the exit. The privately employed professor preceded us by a step or two. His cat-like head, gray and round, just slightly larger than normal, oscillated vaguely, like a dead moon, on his neck. He seemed absent. But finally we heard his proud, muffled voice:

"There was hope. That's how it was."

The restaurant couldn't have been said to be crowded, but in a corner, at the foot of one of those towering walls, was another group that caught the eye: a whole team of soccer players, whom we wouldn't for any reason have expected to encounter there. They had arrived from Zurich and were headed for Rome, and now had just finished a hearty meal. Their powerful, quiet faces, like those of deer or bulls, showed only a total lack of awareness, an obscure muscular triumph. Money seemed to trickle along their limbs like the sweat of a body: they mysteriously glistened with it.

Inspecting them, as he sat along with us at a small table, the privately employed professor seemed to grow even smaller, frailer, more astray in his dreams. His sensitive fingers touched his glass of mineral water with extreme consideration.

"At times, it's nice to eat out. It no longer seems real."

"What no longer seems real?"

"The world we live in: the one that was, and the one to come. We come up against our limits."

"I imagine you're referring to your earnings," said the photographer, offering a slight smile. He was embarrassed.

"That and other things as well. Everything fits so tightly together. My sun isn't the same sun that will shine on all this youthful splendor tomorrow, in Rome or Naples. My sun would sell for twenty-five Lire, fifteen less than a cup of coffee. But I find that quite natural. To be able to explain the classics to one of my students, I don't have to be happy, or in good health. Not at all. I only have to be able to remember, and vividly. So coffee is more important than the sun. The coffee in Milan's cafés is now quite good, and the sun in the city's skies is ever less bright."

"So something's wrong, according to you," said the photographer. "You're talking about an unjust distribution of the sun."

"Of the sun, as of everything else that matters."

"And that's not the way it was before."

"That's the way it has always been. But there was hope, that's what I was trying to say."

"Hope for what?"

"For change. There was pain."

"And now there's no more pain?"

"It's all so private."

"But as far as I can see, we've still got the freedom to complain in public," the photographer laughed.

"There's also the way that the Christ in the paintings in museums complains," the professor said.

"And what do you mean by that?"

"It's a pain that people look at."

"I don't understand," replied the photographer.

"Sir, if I am hungry, here in Italy, that's a part of the landscape. If I lose my wife, here in Italy, that's a problem for the tourist trade. If I walk through overly congested streets, wanting to stand by the sea, if my room is suffocating, if the noises are killing me, if, in a word, I die, that only concerns the national ministry for the preservation of artistic treasures. A citizen's rights, here in Italy, are good for a laugh if they are not accompanied by economic power. In fact, the only true rights are the ones conferred by economic power. So you lose the ability to think; words grow confused and dry up in your throat; and madness is the only thing left as a gentleman's means of proper expression."

For a while the photographer avoided looking at the professor. He wet his lips with the tip of his tongue, as though abashed.

"And it wasn't like this before, in Milan?" he then asked.

"At least not as much as it is today."

He raised a hand and ran it over the surface of the naked wall, from above to below, as though caressing it. His docile eyes momentarily shone with something malignant.

""It's hot," he pleasantly remarked.

"Hot? How do you mean?" said the photographer.

"Hot like hands, like feet. Hot like skin, guts, faces. Like legs, backs. Hot and cold at the same time; weak and thirsty like laboring flesh. Like street cleaners, masons, plasterers, metal workers, salesmen, taxi drivers. Like train engineers, stokers, every kind of factory worker. Like street vendors, shopkeepers, typists, secretaries, teachers. Hot, still hot, forever hot. The streets, the monuments, the squares, the new developments with a splatter of grass, the skyscrapers, the steel and crystal towers, the production machines, the things they produce, the objects of any and every kind in the windows on Via Manzoni: men and women, from the first world war to the second, and from the second to the third, probably; wordless, mute, tamed; with no green trees, no light, no air; all turned into cement, glass, steel; into polishing machines, refrigerators, these people who'd maybe like to have them. Wordless, turned into things; with no arms any more, no hands or faces, but still warm, still hot, food for the growth of industrial civilization. Because industry is hungry; industry has to grow. And what's a human being, tell me, in the face of industry? So that's our God, Chicago, Milan..."

His hand rubbed up and down against wall, and his foot uneasily thumped the ground.

"You're not well," said the photographer, training his eyes on the crazy professor.

"I'm exhausted."

A dry, violent wave of voices came from the soccer players' table, a hard, joyless laughter. Those strong, slightly tottering bodies rose to their feet. Eyes still new and inanimate skimmed over the privately employed professor without taking him in.

"You should try to get help," the photographer said.

"You could hardly be more right, sir."

Immediately afterward, passing a hand across his face as though to shoo away something that bothered him, and with the world's most calm and mysterious voice, the voice of a person talking in a dream, for himself alone:

"That's why I wanted to go to Paris, you see. I always hear that people are respected up there; fair play gets delivered every morning, along with the morning milk. The sun, in the evening, is red from the great fatigue of having shined on everybody. The rivers are there to wash everyone, without discrimination. There's water, freedom, happiness. People who encounter a privately employed professor don't see him as different from anybody else."

"Yes, that's they way I expect it to be," the photographer gently said. And then to the waiter who was passing by: "The bill, please."

The crazy professor had laid a hundred Lire on the table.

"No, no," said the photographer, "let me take care of that."

The professor didn't dare to retrieve his banknote.

"I'll leave it for the dead," he abruptly remarked, with a vague light in his large black eyes, no less turbid than good: the eyes of the mentally ill.

"The dead? Whom do you have in mind?" we asked.

"The dead in general," he quietly responded. "Of Liverpool, Chicago, Milan."

The woman who regarded herself in the mirror of the bar, at eleven o'clock in the evening, in the midst of a crowd of travelers, as well as of the idle and curious (various important trains had just arrived or were just about to leave) was surely no beauty. There was something quite slack in the way she passed a short, heavy hand, the fingernails red, over her hair and around her face, which at once was vulgar and timid, arrogant and grim. Her rose-colored dress said twenty years old, her legs thirty, her arms and shoulders forty. Her torso, on the other hand, no longer had any age at all. Like her face, it had an indistinct air of heaviness and decay. A hard, copper-colored hair-do, streaked with strands of silver, hung down stiffly and artificially on the pink shoulders of her dress.

"Now there's a person who's scared," said the photographer.

"Scared of what?"

"Perhaps of a train that hasn't arrived. But more likely of a client who'll no longer arrive, or if he does she's very tired, and that's all the same thing."

While we observed her, from the rear, she had stopped smoothing her hair and was ordering a cognac.

She drank in quick little sips, with the stupid, single-minded air of a bird, lifting her head with each sip. A darkness hovered on her painted face, between her forehead and her eyes, as though in that region she might have been thinking.

A man, passing behind her, ran a hand down her back:

"Sleepy?"

"Sort of."

The man must have murmured something to her, but she gave absolutely no response, as though only a mosquito had settled onto her ear.

She maintained the dignity and primness, in that frivolous costume, of a senior stenographer of some old firm, a serious worker, much-esteemed, who allowed for no distraction.

"She'll probably pass the night here," the photographer explained to me. "If she doesn't have a record, we'll find her in the waiting room between two and three o'clock, the hour when the restaurant closes for cleaning. But I doubt that they've seen her before. She doesn't have the look of one of the regulars."

It gave us a very strange feeling, on leaving that smoky, somewhat crowded room, to find the station utterly deserted. Suddenly, at times, between one train and another, there's no longer anyone there. The last train for Bologna had left, and there wouldn't be another for a good half hour. Other trains would arrive from Turin, Venice and Genoa, but nothing would depart for at least thirty minutes. The pavement of the concourse was a long, grim mirror of which the surface had something of a stagnant pond. Distant lights reflected on the marble. Beyond the entrance gates to the main platform, the black wings of the cast-iron roofings rose to great heights, spread open like the wings of enormous bats to block out the sky, which could be seen only in the distance where they came to an end: a bruised, purple ring, or an eye full of reddish vapors.

Two policemen, totally in black, perfect and impassive, walked back and forth with automatic stride, up and down the concourse.

They approached us, moved away from us, returned again toward us like shadows, growing larger or smaller.

We asked ourselves where the privately employed professor might be, and the tailor's family, and Luigino, and whether we'd see the woman from the bar again, and toward what city the soccer players were traveling. We also wondered where the Chief Inspector might be. We had spoken with only a few people, but we felt we had listened to everyone, to the whole world, that we had been doing it for years or centuries: their anxieties, the constant lack of something, the effort of rising back to the surface, and the blinding waves. Sleep.

In the waiting room, contrary to our expectation, there were very few people. In the first class waiting room, with its seats that resembled coffins, there was no one at all except a priest.

The photographer was nervous. He laughed, showing his teeth: "Isn't it absurd? There's no one and nothing. Maybe I'm mistaken, but here there's not even emptiness, not even air. Everything is filled with a darkness that holds no oxygen."

The policemen reappeared, framed by the door.

"There's something I begin to wonder about," the photographer remarked.

He added nothing more, but I knew what he was thinking. It was the same obsessive thought that tormented me; a rapidly flickering, secret comparison between these spaces and another: the revelation had been triggered by the sight of the policemen, and by the silence enclosed between these powerful walls, and the scant light.

Its doors weren't barred, but this building was none the less a sealed and secret place.

Our nightmare stemmed from a very real fact.

Seen superficially, this place was a station, but in essence it functioned as a meeting point between an old, obtuse, barbarian Italy and an epoch now hungry for industrial production, on its knees before industrial production and an ever more dizzying quantity of things, of numbers.

One entered this city in order to be turned into things, into numerals, or rejected.

The words of the crazy professor returned to mind: his words on pain as something now forbidden, or in any case illicit. Prohibited pain, and thus the prohibition of the human being. We recalled the few, rare conversations this city had offered; the universal feeling of shame, experienced by all, on every instance of thought or communication, as though they marked a theft from the common good, a monstrous waste of time. We asked ourselves if here—above all here, in its violent attempt to make itself modern, leaping the abysses of pastoral economies and forms of education—Italy wasn't definitively losing its balance, if not plummeting into crisis.

No matter how hard we tried to remember, we wouldn't be able to say how much time slipped by between the moment, observing the policemen, when we abandoned ourselves to these thoughts, and the first hours of the morning.

The station—with its walls and marble floors, its columns, vaults, stairs and still more vaults and halls like frozen rivers—seemed to have lost all weight, all gravity, even its own dismal air: it seemed a rigid, delicate woodcut.

The policemen continued to stroll back and forth, but—perhaps this feeling was due to our tiredness—with a kind of levity, and always more slowly, like the pendulum of a nearly run-down clock.

Travelers, no matter where we went, were now no longer to be seen. Only the oversized brooms of the cleaning crews went back and forth, unhurriedly, with a strange swishing sound: back and forth for hour after hour.

At times we encountered silent little groups: vagabonds, both men and women, waiting for the bar to reopen. Or railroad workers with blackened faces and white eyes, and white teeth, who sat in the halls and smoked a cigarette while waiting for their shift to start.

Even the ceilings spoke only of deserts.

They hung above the endless landing, over the platforms and the gray tracks, like black rain clouds above the bed of a dried-up river.

In the distance, the horizon might have been a hole, or nothing at all; it was empty fog, or maybe stone, and iron poles and wires.

Here and there the blackened figure of a man, a worker or a supervisor: seated in an empty carriage, or on a platform, a siding, head resting on a hand, in silence, staring into the distance.

Were those eyes asleep, or thinking? It was impossible to say, even when they stood wide open.

At a certain hour—it was bitter cold, and the stillness and silence of everything were truly terrible—we headed toward the third class waiting room.

The bad odor, the unhealthy heat, the scant light and the dozens upon dozens of bodies stretched out on the benches, or huddled up, almost as though to protect their heads from the pallor of the lamps, increased that impression of obscurity, secrecy, and abandonment; and the mind grew still more certain of a latent dream or hallucination, which now for several hours, within these walls, this silence, this semi-darkness, had seemed ever more identical with the countenance of the station itself.

From where had those travelers entered this room, and when?

Impoverished men and women who never, in Milan, encounter one another were waiting to depart with the first light of dawn. Coarse peasant skirts, the cotton frocks of the wives of workers, dark shawls and faded, shabby raincoats. Kerchiefs and scarves around their necks and covering their heads.

The faces, in the light, were grave and pallid; sleep carved heavy shadows around the eyes; half-open mouths seemed to be about to speak. The eyes of some stood open, though absolutely motionless. What were they looking at?

We found a seat in a corner, where the naked foot of a child began to brush against our knees.

We saw the mother's dark hands as they pulled him back toward her. But the woman's face, pallid and somber, then went slack, and the tiny foot again stretched out and returned to its prodding.

Seated in front of us were a girl and a boy, embraced, the head of the one resting on the shoulder of the other. The girl wore black stockings, her hair was short and curly, she was dressed in mourning. The boy, perhaps her brother, pale and tranquil as the fog, held her in his arms as he slept. The girl suddenly cried out. "No! no!" she said, waking the boy. She looked around in bewilderment, as though not recognizing where she was.

A face here and there was malign and reckless.

There were also malicious lips, and long, disagreeable hands, obscurely alive.

A few young men were wide awake, pacing back and forth.

Smoking wasn't permitted in the waiting room; the guard, an old gray man, wouldn't allow it. The boys went as far as the door, and struck a match. The reddish light flared briefly in the darkness.

We could not tell, at a certain moment, if we were sleeping or awake, but that spell was then to be broken by a harsh sound of voices. A real, living sound, and strangely painful.

A touch of pink at the entrance to the room shone through the shadows which made it so hard to distinguish the thrown-back faces of the sleeping travelers. It was the woman from the bar, arguing with the guard; she wanted to come it, to sleep. Here are their words:

"You've got no right to keep me from coming in, you know."

"I'd say I do, and that's exactly what I'm up to."

"But it's not fair."

"That's what you say."

"I can go all the way up to the chief of police..."

"Even to God."

Her voice changed, growing desperate and secretive:

"Let me get some sleep."

"First you've got to show me your ticket," replied the man.

"I can't find it.... I must have lost it."

Then laughter. From the man.

When we approached the woman, shortly afterward, since we also needed to take a breath of air, she was leaning, in her fine pink dress and with her aged hair descending onto her shoulders, against a wall, and was watching the dawn.

Her face was calm and opaque, her joyless eyes vaguely searched for something in those vaulted roofings, beyond those vaults, the first gray light which was newly returning. She absorbed the sight and cried.

From so close up, we now saw her hands, which were old and veined. Her body seemed heavy, her make-up was gone, the strands of white stood out in her reddish hair. She had the air of a woman both resolute and finished, caught up in the ancient confusions of the legions of unschooled minds which, in this way or that, are dedicated only to money. Where other women had found their life's solution in running a shop, no less exclusively than blindly, she had found it in another activity, equally exclusive and blind. She must once have been accustomed to living quite well, since the clothes she wore were indeed quite fine, though now worn out. Perhaps her last man had died, or had gotten married and had cut off all assistance. Perhaps she hadn't foreseen a thing like that, and had wasted time. It had been her undoing. On taking a better look at her, at the features below her head of hair, below that horrid skein of pink and white metal, we seemed to glimpse the fresh, clear forehead which she surely had as a girl: the small nose must have been pretty, the pale blue eyes full of joy. As a waitress in a bar, or an office girl for a businessman, perhaps she had had a caller to wait for, in the evenings, before the war; she had surely believed in something—in the warmth of a family, summer suppers, a happy if ingenuous life—or otherwise she wouldn't now have had that aggravated gaze, and no tears would have burned her face.

"Cold?" the photographer remarked.

She made no sign of yes or no, and continued to watch that stony sky.

"It's a bad business, missing a train," the photographer continued, "when it's the last one. You wanted to catch the train for Venice, I guess."

"Venice or Turin," she quietly replied.

"It made no difference?"

"No," she said.

"In here, nothing seems to make a difference any more," the photographer said. "Just the way it is in the rest of the city. But once you get away from it, everything gets back to the way it ought to be."

"Away from it, where?"

"Outside of Milan, even still in Lombardy."

"No. These great tall buildings are everywhere," the woman said. "It gets harder and harder to see a tree. In Bergamo, I had a house in Bergamo; I mean my aunt had a house." The woman corrected herself. "I liked to go there because of the garden. A really big garden, a real garden. They tore it down about a year ago. Now it's a shopping center."

"Leather sells well," the photographer said, "like all the other luxuries, and bread and wine too. But the rivers are in ever worse shape, and the same for the sea, and for everything else that's blue and green."

"You can't breathe," the woman said.

"You can't sleep."

"More and more walls, nothing but walls."

"There are so many people, and nobody."

"Absolutely nobody, no men, no women," said the prostitute.

Suddenly, as she spoke those words, a fear flooded over us. Where were we? And why were we talking with one another? We were strangers. This woman lived outside the law; and we too, in a certain way, placed ourselves outside the law by standing here and talking so freely with her. Yet we didn't break it off. We had the impression of not having talked for centuries, up until tonight: this, after our talk with the crazy professor, was the most sincere conversation in the whole of the capital of Italian industry.

The policemen continued to pass back and forth, and the light increased.

Not sunlight so much as a dull, copper-colored glow at the rear of the highest of the cast-iron roofings. A rusty, copper brightness, at moments pinkish, always murky, but expanding. The shadows beneath those vaults, those arches, those enormous portals, that iron, that smoke, those sheets of glass, moment by moment receded, revealing dusty, dark, inert materials. The reflections that flashed from the tracks grew colder. From the tracks, from the motionless wagons, from the gates, the marble, the glass, the iron. The returning light came in the company of a sudden, burgeoning hum of a different kind of sound, no longer belonging to the world of sleep, but flushed already with haste and renewed anxiety, with feverishness. A boy shouted a newspaper headline, all the lights of the kiosks suddenly turned on, a small crowd of people stood in front of the tobacco stands.

People came in a row up the great stairs, carrying suitcases.

The woman's face, right there beside us, had grown mysteriously distant. Closed up in itself, absent, guarded by an absolute solitude, like the solitude of the dead, it no longer had any weight; and offered no replies, no questions; only a tiny smile, and a strange fog in the hollow of the eyes.

Then, discretely, the sound of her heels as she walked away.

We will never, after tonight, meet her again; not in this life, and not in this city, nor in any other. But those footsteps, and that silence, everywhere.

"Nothing, that's what's going on," came the calm reply of another voice.

We too looked toward the gates that separate the concourse from the main platform, and we had to admit that something, over there, in a scant few minutes, had profoundly changed.

The deserted sidings of not very long before had exploded into a wave of life.

It still remained obscure; a dark mass in the dim light, teeming vaguely in the shadow of a train which a moment earlier had not been there; a force still fluid, vague, and silent, and yet violent. Rapidly it burst toward the gates, narrowed to find its way through them, then swelled again and erupted in all directions.

Then we saw individual people, ever more people, and still more people. We heard their brief, tight voices, and the way they breathed. Men, and women as well, young and old. They wore no smiles, showing nothing but serious, sunken, sleepy faces. A few of them began to pass in front of us, but seemed nearly to lack all solidity, like shadows, in flight. Shortly afterward, another wave surrounded another train, thronged at the gates, and reinforced the first. Then a third, a fourth, and others again. "Workers" said a voice not far away from us.

A gray sea of people that beat at dawn against the shores of the Lombard capital, biting its stone, assailing its stone and metal prodigies. At evening they withdrew, like a sad sea, and scattered into the hinterland, to fill the dark with their breathing. The next day at dawn, they reappeared: this was the city's only sea, its human sea, the tidal breathing of the city of Milan.

Men; young men, almost boys; boys, still almost babies. The adolescent who bites into a piece of bread while running; the young man, or almost old, who while running stamps out the butt of his cigarette; the woman who seems distressed as she hurriedly wraps her scarf around her neck. They are late; they got up late; they wanted to sleep a moment longer; and now they run to catch their trolley.

A boy in front of us trips and falls. For a moment we touch his thin, cold hands (they might have been the claws of a lifeless bird) and he responds with an unseeing glance.

"We can't stop, we can neither stop nor talk," was the message of those pale blue eyes.

No one stopped, not even for an instant; no one exchanged a word with a neighbor. Eyes turned only to one or another of the great clocks.

They launched themselves down the stairs, and seemed to roll or tumble, like dark water into a gulch, descending to who knows where; and disappeared.

Then it was daytime, and all of them were gone.

Milan had begun a new day; the Central Station—gateway to labor, bridge of necessity, estuary of simple blood—had absolved and brought to an end its one true function: as a link which connects an eternal supply of labor to an equally eternal and impassive metropolis.

The columns, the bas-reliefs, the winged lions; the vaulted roofs, the bars, the smoke; the stone and the iron, the white and the black, the horrid "thing" in Piazza Duca d'Aosta, once again reverted to an honest backdrop: to silence, an abstraction.

Nebel (A Lost Story)

The central hall, or drawing room, of *I Portici*—the country home of Princess Giuliana d'Ajala, at the lower edge of the woods that dominate the tiny town of Amalfi—was growing bright, just as it had done for more than forty years, with the sinister fires of sunset. At the very same moment that the sun descended behind a stand of trees, the splendid light it cast within the room would seem in fact to harshen, and a violet blue would mix with its divinely springtime reds and honeys. Antique brocades, bronzes, mirrors, all the Indian and Chinese vases, the majolica, the consoles, the enameled doors, everything was briefly flooded with a wounded light which almost flared—after an instant when it seemed quite dead—and then shimmered, waned, and disappeared.

Almost simultaneously, the enchanting sound of a bell flowered—"flowered" is the right word, since everything at that moment had the levity of summer vegetation—in the courtyard before the house, which was planted with beds of flowers, but where horses and carriages, in accordance with old, rustic custom, might stop. Princess Giuliana, reclining on a pale blue sofa by the open window, immediately cast a glance at her friend Rosanna Di Berto, a simple bourgeoise, who was seated on a low chair beside her, smoking uninterruptedly. The princess informed her, just barely winking her left eye (which happened to be a bit less blue than the right one) that Baron von Nebel had probably arrived.

The baron—if for no other reason than the vast boredom and spirited banter which sometimes teem in the calm of summer vacations, when vacations are very rich and secluded, and by virtue as well of his being the princess' nephew, somewhat distantly—had been expected for over a week by her guests at *I Portici*. These guests were the Dukes of Caserta, man and wife, quite young, and already on the verge, it was whispered, of divorce; the young Roffo Alliani, a lawyer, an intellectual, and a "match" still actively contended by the young ladies of society; and finally Father De Biase, a fine and discriminating Jesuit who had come up from Amalfi to *I Portici* just the previous night, hoping to arrange with the prince to consult a few papers in his archives, whereas the prince had gone to Naples to see off at the airport an American niece who had passed through briefly with her husband. Rosanna Di Berto was likewise a member of this affable group of guests, even if her presence was always the case when the princes resided at *I Portici*, which is to say almost habitually, since between them had arisen—between the young Rosanna, bourgeois and straightforward, and the aged, most noble Giuliana—one of those ardent friendships, nearly a love affair, which are not at all infrequent among privileged people. And perhaps it found its explanation in the great importance which both of these ladies had ascribed, and continued to ascribe, to matters of the heart; for it was said of Giuliana that she had been lucky in love (as her beauty declared), and the opposite might have been said of Rosanna; and this—since contraries seek each other out—might have furnished the basis for their delectable, reciprocal fealty to one another.

So for a whole week, with the further complicity of a gorgeous moon which, waxing, adorned a likewise growing May, the focus of discussion in that little circle had been the youthful German whose carriage—a true curiosity in these times of the automobile—seemed now to announce itself with the sound of the bell. Not that Claus Nebel was a figure of any greatness; he owned no more than a property, left him by an aunt, on the hills of Sorrento, and a sprawling mansion in Baviera, his country of origin. Curiosity followed wherever he went perhaps because of the very fact that Neapolitan society spoke really quite little about him. He was so close to insignificant, or contrived to appear insignificant as a way of escaping the pigeon-holes held always ready by the outside world; he seemed intent on subtracting his life and interior substance—whatever it might have been—from any attempt to define them. So, even though it appeared quite clear, at least to the prince, that Claus was a man of scant imagination and coarse spirit, the gossip of the momentarily assembled guests at *I Portici* had endowed his face, his acts, and his figure, which was said to be quite handsome, with an interest and a grace of which the baron himself would have had no expectation.

Only the two ladies and the servants were present in the villa, since earlier in the afternoon the Dukes of Caserta and Roffo Alliani had gone to the villa of the latter, near Vietri; and Father De Biase, on a visit to the dean of Amalfi, wouldn't return until late in the evening.

"Really? By carriage?" Rosanna Di Berto inquired of her friend, she too having caught the tinkle of the approaching bell. Her surprise had brought three creases to her brick-colored forehead, and added at least thirty years to her age.

Instantly—as the princess lightly placed a hand on her shoulder, almost as though to say "let's see" (Giuliana was equally incredulous, though surely not because of the carriage)—the young woman stood up, nervously smoothing her straw-colored sweater against her hips and then, with a thoughtful air, tucking back into place a large lock of flame-colored hair. Her nose, in the midst of a mannish face, was somewhat prominent; and her ugliness, if that's what we wish to call it, was made more grave by the smallness of her stature, by her short, strong legs, and by a pair of beautiful but unfortunately masculine hands; she also had a willful personality and a virile intelligence. She was already thirty-two, and by now, in spite of her joking tone on the subject, had despaired of marrying. So her spirits, on hearing that Nebel was in the courtyard, turned grim.

The sound of the bell had meanwhile splintered and faded; nothing more of it remained than a hovering echo, of the substance of a sigh. The hushed whisper of the wheels of the carriage had likewise lapsed, leaving only a soft creaking of springs. Then, Giuseppe, the oldest of the prince's three servants entered the drawing room, announcing Nebel.

"Claus," Giuliana contentedly called out.

The baron was already advancing into the room.

His mother, a noblewoman, before becoming the widow of a simple baron, and then of a banal Herr Strauss, had been an intimate friend of Giuliana, who now was seventy years of age. She had been a haughty woman, of fairly disagreeable manners, and of habits—while twice waiting to reachieve her freedom, and ever more unhappily—which had been very liberal and disorderly, whereas Giuliana was the very personification of detached discretion and composure. Of his mother the son had acquired not so much the height, as rather the perfect proportions of figure, and the inborn elegance. He had a very calm and handsome face, with a soldier's forehead, surmounted by thick brown hair; his nose was short, and his eyes, intensely blue, were anything other than closely set. As he approached Giuliana he smiled, and a kind of light condensed on his brow. He then kissed the hand of Rosanna as well, but he didn't seem to see her, or to take the slightest interest in her.

"My dear," the princess joyously said, "I am so happy, believe me, that you are here." And turning to Rosanna: "Here, dearest, we have a man of legend...for the simple fact that he escapes all legend. It would be difficult in Naples to find a man more modest or stingy of charm than Nebel. Which is where his charm most resides!"

She brought her fine, radiant face—miraculously free of the tiniest wrinkle—to the face of Claus, and placed her well-turned hands on his shoulders:

"You won't get away so quickly, my boy," she said. "We'll do everything we can to keep you."

"I'm sorry, Giuliana," Claus began, "tomorrow evening..."

"I know, I can imagine your excuses. But I am not resigned..."

And the old woman surveyed the young man, lovingly, between laughter and tears.

Claus lowered his admirable brown head, and a straight, thin wrinkle formed between his black eyebrows; in that moment, his blue eyes, in which nothing was inscribed—or things that never, ever again would rise to the surface—turned almost black, and there was something in his manner, in those solid shoulders, in the beauty of his clouded brow, that wounded Rosanna, so subtly and profoundly as to force her to take a step backward. She had been struck by her own small poverty; and the baron's magnificence, which she clearly dis-cerned, was reason to despise him. Again in that very moment, he turned his dark, unquestioning gaze in her direction.

"Certainly it is wonderful here...."

"And truly a shame that in your wanderings you have taken no thought to profit from it."

"Wanderings, aunty?" That was the affectionate term with which Nebel addressed the princess in their moments of greatest tenderness. "But there is so much I have to do!" And again he looked at Rosanna, as though espying behind her another person he vaguely recognized. The glance ebbed away. "You know that my wife has caused me a great many worries," he quietly added.

"The property?"

The princess was well-informed as to how things stood. The luxuries and follies of Clara von Nebel—the cold blonde whom Claus had married ten years previously—had already squandered a good part of Claus' wherewithal. Aside from the villa in Baviera, he was left with only a large grove of oranges and a house in Sorrento, purchased a bit before the war and since then greatly increased in value, arriving, so it seemed, to as much as eighty million Lire. But the baroness wanted to cede it for a far smaller sum to those very same Americans, relatives of the Ajalas, whom the prince the previous evening had gone to see off in Naples. With the always adamant demand that he give her satisfaction, she had kept Claus virtually besieged, chiding what she called his miserly attitude.

"You don't mean to say you've sold it?" queried Giuliana, suddenly serious and taking a backwards step while looking at him fixedly, almost with pity, almost as though to confide that she grasped the sharpness of his pain, since indeed she had read the cruel reply in her young friend's lowered eyes.

"I'm afraid I have."

"But Carlo,"—Carlo was the prince's name—"has told me nothing."

"It was only last night," Nebel explained, seating himself on the pale blue divan and throwing back his shoulders with that militaresque simplicity which everyone envied in him; and the ladies, not at all surprised by this liberty, lent him their full attention. "Carlo," he continued "spent the day at the sailing club, and afterwards his number at the beach house was always busy. Winter, in the meantime, had phoned me again, raising his offer from sixty to seventy million. Take it or leave it, since, as you know, they were flying that evening to New York. I had a moment not of weakness, but of serious reflection. Clara had already unbuttoned herself as to what this money might mean for her, and for me as well."

"Which is to say?" Giuliana responded.

Claus rubbed two fingers against his eyes and briefly wiped his forehead. "Which is to say that she'll be able to return to New York, for good, and that I will have no further obligations to her. That's quite convenient for me; the best I could hope for."

"And you? What about you?"

"I, aunty, am still in my thirties," Claus serenely replied. "And I have my degree in languages. Greek, Latin, English, German...and even a bit of Sanskrit...." He released a short burst of brittle laughter. "I face no lack of possibilities. And when I'm old, if it comes to that, I'll go back to Baviera."

"Ah, how sad! Ah, the things you have to make me listen to!" Giuliana d'Ajala softly repeated, with a pity that amounted more than anything else to tenderness and maternal admiration. And she had forgotten Rosanna, who, meanwhile, embarrassed by her unintentional lack of discretion, attempted to assume a distant air while going about to turn on a light here and there. "Rosanna, please, would you ring for tea? Thank you, my dear. You, my Claus, have acted nobly, with that disregard for gain which all of us admire without having the courage to practice it. But you'll allow me to say that you have gone this time much further than prudence would have counseled. Rosanna, my dear, say instead that tea is no longer required. It is almost evening, and dinner isn't very far off. Rather, my dears, take an aperitif." She herself went to fetch the cart. While extracting glasses from its lower shelf, she asked, looking toward Claus:

"Has the agreement already been signed?"

"Yes, of course. A lawyer was present. But the transfer of title must still, of course, be registered."

"And the furniture? All your splendid furniture?" Giuliana again inquired, while pouring, from the bottle Rosanna had indicated, port—instead of vermouth—which shone with the color of a dark ruby. Claus too had asked for port, but he wasn't drinking, and the somber fingers he wrapped about the glass seemed to share his effort of reflection.

"Clara will have a part of them, and I as well. For the rest, I don't really know. I imagine I'll arrange a sale."

"But have you already found a flat?"

"I have seen a place in Naples that would do."

"So you'll be setting yourself up in Naples?"

"I imagine so." Claus paused. "I'll go back to giving lessons, just as I did as a student, and I'll have more time for my own studies. To your health, aunty!"

"To yours, my dear."

Giuliana rapidly clinked her glass against her nephew's.

She was moved. Claus seemed calm. Rosanna, she too with a glass in her motionless hands, observed them.

Rosanna had reacted with the silence she shared with all women whose lives have fallen repeatedly short of their secret aspirations, ceaselessly wounding their pride: with a silence which had turned, as years went by, into a certain gravity, and which had brought her the gift (perhaps the bitter gift) of a heightened spirit of observation. She saw and understood much more than her circle of friends and confidantes might presume. Indeed, she had had to learn to govern her heart, so as to keep it from seeing and feeling too much, and from shaping all the attendant reflections, for she had noted how often the truth about persons and facts is far from nice, even without the knowledge of the persons in question, and how her gift for discovering the disappointing truth of reality—even in the most fantastic forms that reality sometimes assumes, almost as though in defense of its insignificance—brought no consolation into her life. She had acquired the art of prudence, which, in its spiritual form, is compassion for oneself and the world; and most likely her friendship with Giuliana d'Ajala was so perfect because each of these women had understood—the one thanks to time, the other to ugliness—that life has nothing fine about it if not a certain azure atmosphere, deprived of which it turns into nothing but a senseless bubbling of gasses. And that atmosphere was furnished by the feelings and their properly nurtured appearances—since the feelings can fill and conceal the abyss with the flowers and colors of harmonious conversation.

Now, while this rapid and apparently banal conversation was taking place between Giuliana and the young baron, Rosanna, having grown sadder of heart than she normally was, since Claus and the nearing May night had laid siege to her poverty, allowed little sparks to move through her mind, like lightning bugs in the hay, advancing, wavering, flickering out, and then suddenly flashing anew. Rather than reflections, which couldn't have formed in her rigid trance, these lightning bugs were impressions and perceptions of a reality which Rosanna found less datable, but also more real, even though obscure, than the present. Its nucleus was the unmistakable affection that Giuliana felt for her nephew. Suddenly, however, as she watched the princess' almost god-like face flood with beneficent light while beholding the visage of Claus, Rosanna forced herself to respect her friendship with Giuliana, and bemusedly asked herself whether, owing to Claus, and thus to a wholly external fact, she wasn't in the course of betraying it. With entirely instinctive resolution (her greatest strength) she therefore assumed a light and casual manner, and with a banal excuse—she must make a phone call—left the room.

Her intention, at first, was to return to her little room on the upper floor of *I Portici*. Then, since her feelings were awry and she wished to reason clearly, she decided instead to go out into the garden.

To reach this marvelous garden, which spread out from the flanks of the house like the wings of a giant butterfly, she had to cross a vast open space which divided into two parts. The first, adjacent to the building's facade, was terraced, whereas the second was the courtyard true and proper, graded with minute gravel, brightened here and there by small pink stones.

The evening hour had deprived the atmosphere of its usual luminosity, that sheen of bright celeste which counted as its most distinctive beauty. The sky now held a note of green and a scattering of violet vapors, from which there arose, to the right and left, the sublime panorama of the Amalfi coast: a great, single orange grove beneath bald mountains where high, rose-colored gullies still lay in mysterious sunlight. The distant sea was only a strip of uncertain light, a powdery blue, and might have seemed a prairie. It was hidden, moreover, by a more tumultuous sea of boughs and leaves, and thin contorted trunks: the stand of olives in which the Ajalas took such pride.

Nature, for Rosanna, was of nearly no interest at all, a closed book, as it is for most women, despite their refinement, and as dictated, more than anything else, by our time's spirit of realism. So even though these forms and colors—which she didn't see as existing on their own, but rather as emanations of a sentimental sensibility—held an air of mystery which disturbed her, she focused her attention only upon those things which were able to offer her relief. The air blew in from that world of greenery and salty water and brushed her head like a friendly caress; the somber color of the sky brightened the moon and various stars; these things were familiar, and soothed rather than stirred her thoughts.

She proceeded to the edge of the courtyard, thinking to continue on to the garden's principal alleyway, which, instead of opening out, became at a certain point a modest, fanciful, country lane, spiraling down, bend after bend, protected here and there by a drystone wall, to the city below. It wasn't that she thought of prolonging her stroll to the garden's lower limits, but she wanted to reach the start of that path, and then turn back. Instead, before having advanced as much as a hundred steps, she saw her route blocked by a glossy, blue shadow, which she recognized, though she had never seen it before, as Claus' carriage.

It was a lean, yet antiquated one-horse Tilbury. The horse, white and very calm, was hitched to a tree by a thin red lanyard and made no other sound, in this place of motionless serenity, than the vague quiver of its breathing and the rhythmic rustle of its tail, which now and then flicked against the carriage's forward edge. Rosanna halted a little distance away, but not so far away as to prevent the animal's gaze from communicating a certain sweetness to her. It seemed a stream of diamonds springing from a vortex, which was the horse's eye. And in that particular moment, she gave no thought, nor could she have, to the oddness of a carriage in a place which, yes, so elegant, was nonetheless—like every other corner of the world, except perhaps for archaic countrysides buried and left behind by time—equipped with garages and motorcars. She coupled it in her mind with Claus' tame and yet imperious beauty, with that manner he had, both immediate and remote; and though it was surely no triumph of logic, she explained it as a taste for the antiquarian, which accounted moreover for the gravity and somewhat funereal grace of the man.

Inside this two-seater, among the fine leather cushions, one noticed, perfectly forgotten, an old rawhide bag which seemed to be quite empty. But from one of its pockets, which hadn't been buckled, and which perhaps had flipped opened as the carriage bounced along the path, there emerged a volume bound in black or dark blue, very worn, and Rosanna, who had seen an identical volume in her father's studio, when he had still been alive, had no difficulty identifying it. Looking aslant at the gilded eyes which spelled out the letters of the title—eyes which stared back into her own—she recognized the *Confessions* of Saint Augustine.

Despite its binding, the book had the air of something retrieved from the rubbish. Its pages were swollen and grubby like those of a magazine or a newspaper which had passed from hand to hand; and what inspired a kind of horror in Rosanna was the thought that this infinite number of hands, in the present case, amounted to *only two*. Then she fancied that the book probably didn't belong to Claus, but to the prince, from whom Claus would have borrowed it merely out of curiosity, intrigued by the age of the edition, and to whom he intended to return it this evening. That thought calmed the young woman, who, once again, as though seeking some further reassurance, cast a glance at the mare, and again she was struck by that stream of diamonds, which descended nearly like tears from the creature's black eyes.

The dinner bell sounded, and Rosanna, without any hurry, since she expected no relief from this meal, made her way back across the courtyard and re-entered *I Portici*.

Like the whole of the Ajalas' villa, the dining room reflected the exquisite spirit of a convent, set off as it was from the other first-floor rooms—the drawing room, the library, the music room—by a low, simple, open archway, defended by only a curtain of Havana satin which was usually gathered back. The four rooms flowed one into another with a sense of ideal continuity. The furniture, here, in contrast to the drawing room, was simple and sober. A rectangular table, tall inlaid chairs, a precious fourteenth-century crucifix on the wall. In the other rooms—the library and the music room—there was not a great deal more, aside from the books and the piano. The windows, however, were splendid; they were arched, and they embodied the most profound and exquisite beauty which the house had to offer. During the day they were filled with all of nature's colors, with every gradation of blue and green, and at night they became a candid frame for the blackness of the cosmic abyss, exclusively traversed by light and brilliant caravans of stars. Among them, on summer nights, the Great Bear's chariot, as though in a jeweled vitrine, might have been the rarest pendant. One easily imagined the Ajalas' grand pride, their regal yet unassuming manner, to derive not only from blood, but as well, perhaps, from the splendid home in which they had chosen to live toward the end of their lives; it allowed them a certainty of who knows quite what exorbitant glory and immortality, beyond the coming dissolution of their glory as human beings.

A bland light, cast by two lamps affixed to facing walls, shed an enormous clarity onto the dazzling whiteness of the table linen, all the better revealing the lunar grace of the porcelain plates, the muted glow of the silver, the undersea splendor of the crystal goblets.

The dinner was entirely modest: a soufflé of potatoes, salad, an omelet. But all of it, along with the fruit, was prepared and served in ways that made it clear that this was a princely modesty.

Giuliana had certainly had no time to change, and her attire, moreover, was so exquisite—she wore her favorite color, a white which caught the highlights of her snowy hair, gathered across her forehead and fixed at the nape of her neck as a kind of natural prolongation of her noble, cameo-like head—as to make one think that the scarf of finest silver-threaded wool which she had rested on her shoulders constituted a new ensemble. In her delicate, rose-toned face, offered like a human flower to the clarity of the lamps, there reposed a deeper sweetness which Rosanna, on entering the room, saw as resembling that flush of violet which had colored the sunset, perhaps an hour earlier. She held her hands clasped beneath her chin, her wrist was adorned with only a bracelet of pearls, and she was fixing Claus with the ageless, radiant, vaguely grave expression which accounted for the fame of her

Dutch lady's eyes. Blue, manly eyes, the eyes of a sailor, so ardent and potent, and yet crossed by the mortal compassion of a dove. She had that power which accrues to women of age, and eternally smiling lips as well, which made that power always acceptable and comprehensible. Claus, already seated and still somewhat distracted when Rosanna entered the room, rose for a moment to his feet at the entrance of Giuliana's friend and turned a nervous smile to the young woman.

"Please excuse me..." the princess' friend began, a little inwardly.

"My dear, you have no cause to excuse yourself," the matron abruptly replied. She had shifted, as she often would do, and especially in these more recent times, from the familiar *tu* to the gelid *voi*, which seemed a caprice, or might have been due to rapidly shifting humors. "The air, outside, is quite mild; and Claus and I are slightly melancholy, so we were hardly thinking of eating at all."

"Me, *melancholy?*" the baron remarked with vague surprise, pulling back his shoulders. "No, I wouldn't say so. I'm not even tired." But while speaking he threw a glance at Rosanna which belied these words—as though her ugliness reassured him—with a more fatigued humanity, with a kind of general pardon. Rosanna waited anxiously for this glance to prolong or repeat itself, but instead it subsided, and disappeared.

"Your youth, Claus, deceives you. You are not so strong as you imagine yourself to be, believe me," the princess retorted, while spreading her brocaded napkin. "You'll have to allow a woman of my years, if indeed they still permit me to be seen as a woman at all, and not simply as the bark of a tree shattered by the lightning of time, to realize just how tired you are and to recognize the pain that courses across your skin. Yes, dear Claus, the very skin of your body is everywhere in pain, in a circumstance like this, and not only your boyish heart. Yet you attempt to deceive yourself, instead of allowing the free flow of tears which would surely serve you better."

She looked back at Rosanna, as though asking for amicable concurrence; and then, again regarding Claus: "My friend Rosanna, who now sits here between us, must cause you no embarrassment. Her difficult youth has taught her the art of graceful indifference; so even while here with us, she is now at quite some distance away. Isn't that so, Rosanna?"

"I wouldn't much want to talk about other possibilities, and, indeed, this evening I am very tired," Rosanna responded. "I wonder, in fact, if the tranquilizers I usually take ought not to be changed."

Rosanna's words were mainly intended to show disinterest, and thus to lighten the weight of the conversation's prior secrecy. Both Giuliana and the baron were grateful.

"You use tranquilizers!" remarked Claus, relieved by this unexpected lack of interest; and he regarded the girl as though replying to a voice of uncertain origin. And Rosanna felt his distance and nonchalance so intensely as to suffer a twinge a pain. She tried to catch the gaze of his dark eyes, but all she found was the same unruffled vagueness as before, which she read as an indication of an instinctive antipathy.

"As well as many other medicines," she added with hidden sarcasm. "But medicines, in the lives of modern women and men, are an indispensable balm…"

"For what?" Nebel promptly inquired.

"An ingenuous question, my boy," Giuliana interrupted, "and even though I am not an expert on human pain, since I have wisely avoided it, I'm aware of the principal source of your own. You think that nature, in which we too are immersed, is sound; you imagine that it's pure and incorruptible, and that we could save ourselves by returning to it. But that's not the way things stand. Only reason and the profound study of the human body and the way it functions, and a knowledge of the forces, internal and external, which are able to destroy it, only that can offer a modicum of security and therefore of hope."

"Excuse me, aunty, but our friend, just a moment ago, spoke of an 'indispensable balm.' And in spite of your luminous quickness of mind, you still have not answered my question as to what the pain would be for which that balm proves indispensable. What, according to you, or in the lady's opinion, is the nature of this pain from which one has to seek relief? I don't at all see it, or it contradicts natural logic, and indeed would spring from reason's being overwhelmed by its opposite. If the human condition is the only condition in which human beings can find themselves, what then would be the source of this disturbance, this pain, which forces us to search for a cure, for a way of 'tranquilizing' ourselves? And if it isn't, why then don't we simply return to wherever we were before? Why ask tranquilizers for an artificial surrogate of that sleep, or dream, which initially—you too admit it—made for the peace of mind and the highest good of women no less than men?"

A perturbed but no less ironic smile flowered onto Giuliana's lips.

"I am happy to note," she countered, "your haughtiness, and, in a certain sense, your aggressive dialectic, my boy. It's the proof, so to speak, of your youth. But you mustn't imagine to have trapped me in the nets of your subterranean argumentation. I can see the source of its violence even though you'd like to hide it from me." She lowered her untroubled eyes. "Life, Claus, will teach you that all this strangeness—as human life appears to you to be—isn't strange at all. Yes, our curiosity and useless questions quite truly make the human being the Achilles' heel of reality, where all things live within the limit of renewing and repeating themselves in a kind of divine sleep, which is something to which we cannot return. Our sickness lies in the constant growth of the mind, in our constant understanding, in this listening, this vigilance. You and I and a very few others sip only the nectar of culture and self-awareness, whereas the masses are exposed to their cruelty and horror. So, today we look out at all of nature's divine grandeur—and nature, even where she has wounded herself, restitches and licks her own wounds—we look out around us and what we see is the rebirth of a kind of tame animality, everywhere. The animal sleeps; and humans too, like animals, want to sleep. That, Claus, is the quality of our century. And medicines—since conversation is denied to the masses—lead even the common people back to that dreamless sleep to which they aspire."

At that moment, Domenico, one of the domestics, appeared in the doorway to announce, with the timid voice of an ex-peasant, that Father De Biase, by telephone from Amalfi, begged to be excused for his delay, and would like to know if the baron had arrived.

"You see him here before you, my dear!" remarked the ancient lady, delighting in her own sardonic tone. "Tell him," she added, "that the baron is here. And remind the good Father that we expect his arrival later this evening."

"The Reverend Father has told me that he's almost certain he won't be able to make it; but he'll be here tomorrow."

"Then tell him we'll expect him tomorrow."

Domenico disappeared, and Claus, who upon hearing the Jesuit's name had nearly risen to his feet and betrayed an expression of anxiety, as though fearing that the Father had arrived at the villa, resumed his former manner: he was once again a guest intent on nothing but intelligent conversation. Yet his start had not escaped the silent Rosanna, who, coupling the discovery of the book with Claus' brief alarm at the name of Father De Biase, thought for a moment that perhaps the baron's depth was nothing more than a banal Catholic depth—and who was to say that the subtle De Biase hadn't been Claus' friend and confessor, more than simply his Latin teacher, during his studies at the Istituto Pontano? As a boy, the baron had in fact studied in Naples, and his mother had been Catholic.

"Claus, you should really have a taste of this Bordeaux. Roffo brought it last month," the princess remarked, filling a small glass and offering it to her nephew.

"You know I don't drink, aunty...at least not usually."

"And you make a great mistake. Judicious use of alcohol is just the right way to compensate.... Tell me Claus, are you well acquainted with Don Igino De Biase? Does he interest you, I mean *particularly?* I find him quite pleasant and discreet. A man, as they say, who is full of human kindness. Or by now do you disapprove of him?"

"No," Claus answered, at least partly giving support with these words to Rosanna's suppositions, "certainly not as a professor at the lyceum. As a man of the world, I couldn't say. That's what I'll learn tomorrow when I see him." He then explained to Giuliana that one of his reasons for accepting her invitation to *I Portici* lay in his desire to see his old teacher again. He had written him, and had learned he'd be staying at *I Portici* until Saturday.

Rosanna was wholly an atheist, and to stay awake while listening to this conversation required a special effort of the will. Only one fact cheered her: the brusque emotion she had felt on Claus' arrival seemed to have lessened. As she listened to his talk, she had to agree with the prince that the whole of his intelligence was anchored to a desperate paltriness. Here was a man who had just put an end, no more than twenty-four hours ago, to every further possibility of giving or receiving anything from his wife, a man who had renounced the proud distinction of being Clara's husband. Yes, one could think her a woman of whom there might be much to question, but she was gifted with great personality and he must have loved her, and now she was carting away his past. He had thrown it all up with such satisfied, actuarial precision; and now he prepared—without so much as a sigh, a tremor, or a fear—to resume an arid, solitary life, as though returning to his natural state; he was ready, moreover to look for solace in the company of priests, in scholastic discussions of good and evil, which are truly such sordid discussions when a person is capable of neither. It sent a chill straight through her. This cold, indeed, was the feeling to which Rosanna was most accustomed, and Claus' arrival had done no more than to set it awry for a moment, exposing her instead to confusing illusions; so the sentiments the young man now aroused in her held a shade of impatience, even of hatred. Nearly suspecting that this feeling had materialized, and wondering whether he could feel its ice, she cast a sidelong glance in his direction, again to be astounded and almost enthralled by the dark, blue light of his eyes, which peered toward the window, as if that were where the answer lay.

She watched his perfect hands, of a pale nut-brown color, quiver ever so slightly against the pallor of the tablecloth, and then open in a sign almost of resignation, or of waiting.

At that moment—going on nine o'clock—a singular silence hung over the house and all the space around it.

It was utterly clear, even if everything reflected the quiet of a night at the end of May or the start of June, that the countryside surrounding *I Portici*—the countryside and the starry sky and the weak and very pure wind that played through the leaves of the olive trees, or in the rose garden below the terrace—had leant no ear to these people's conversation; that these human judgments in no way touched them; and that silent nature contained a force of its own; a ferment, a dream, a splendor. It contained a cry of ecstasy, and also an endless demonstration that stretched beyond these human discussions, much as the *peep peep peep* of a family of sparrows in a nest is annulled by the wave of all the birds in the universe, and of the woods in which they live, the seas they cross, the cosmic lights from which they take their colors. And the baron's eyes appeared to be no stranger to this awareness, both certain and desperate, of forms of existence that lie beyond the human, and which are more profound, much more profound. Those eyes seemed to hold the replies of a son, a motion of abandon against that breast, a horrible headlong rush.

The princess too seemed to be aware of it, and she glanced at Rosanna, and then at Claus, timidly, showing her courageous smile. Then, having folded her napkin, she rose, since dinner was over. She asked if Claus would like coffee, and on hearing that he wouldn't she rang for Domenico to bring it to Rosanna and herself. The two young people had likewise risen to their feet, and the group was proceeding through the archway, to the drawing room, when from not very far away, indeed from quite close by, there resounded a brief and somehow muffled whinny.

"Claus! We have forgotten your horse! Such an enchanting voice! We're being scolded!" the old woman lovingly remarked, as her face brightened. She placed a hand on the young man's shoulder: "I'll send Domenico!"

"I'll go myself, instead," said Claus, his phrase unadorned by the "would you mind?" which a minimum regard for proper form would clearly have required. And rapidly, with a taut and trembling face, incredibly perturbed, he crossed the drawing room and left. Shortly thereafter, his footsteps sounded rapidly off toward the carriage.

Alone again with one another, the two women exchanged a sudden, charitable glance. They rediscovered their friendship in the way, once again, in which they had been moved—despite themselves, and regardless of any judgment they might have made—by the presence of a man who, more than any other they knew, might merit that name.

The naiveté, the purity, and as well the violence that constituted the very substance of Claus von Nebel had bewitched them, and they had no way to say so if not with the rapid squeeze of a hand that grasped another, the deeply moved hand of the old woman on the pained hand of the young one....

It's here that the tale of Nebel breaks off in this Lost Story, *though in fact the* Story *was lost in only one sense: in the sense that what took place from the moment in which the baron left the room was not ascertained and tran-*

scribed: these events reached the author's ear only by way of gossip and rumor, and conscience insisted that the author maintain silence. For if the merry chorus of Amalfi's speculations was lightly accepted (as indeed it was generally accepted), the story grew vaguely frightening and might have done damage to the repu-tations of persons—like the baron and his aunt (and as well the unhappy Rosanna)—who were irreprehensible and good. (The thought that goodness is not always irreprehensible, as people tend to believe, belongs to a different train of considerations.) So perhaps it's for the better that the story was lost. And, surely, no earthly or heavenly power will ever be able to re-weave the thread of those affectionate divagations. This is something of which the person who notes their irreparable disappearance not only from a drawer, but from all the drawers of life—if not for those of sad and wayward memory—is fully aware. So the only thing to do is to offer one's apologies to the Reader who may one day encounter these pages and then be called up short before the rapid squeeze of the hand exchanged between the two women, the ancient and gorgeous Giuliana and the hard and unhappy modern young woman. A voice had marked the night—a non-human voice—and alarmed the silence with the depth of its tenderness, which came from another world, an entirely different world.

Where, with advancing night, were they going, these alert and inquiring minds at I Portici? *Who could say, after so much time? The story of these various voices and lives that moved through a spring just after the war, and which said and feared something monstrous, some-thing that inverted and altered the very meaning of the trial so recently undergone, presenting all notions of the victory of reason as charged with illusion and error—a thesis we are surely far from sharing—stops here; and the rumors and gossip (frequently ignoble) of Amalfi's clubs, which prolonged the fascination of its secret, can offer no more than externals.*

A trace, however, even if scumbled and quickly contradicted, of what followed up until the moment when the baron suddenly departed from I Portici *six hours later (the stars by then had changed their places, it was dawn, which visits those mountains a little bit earlier than in any other locale) can be discerned in the declarations made by Father Igino De Biase (Nebel's former professor of Greek and Latin at the Istituto Pontano) a week or so later to friends of his in Grenoble, who received him, in no less comfort than severity, like the very tribunal of Man's most intimate substance: "...such a kind and gentle mind," he said, "...no one might have imagined that such a rebellion lay within him. I can say nothing more.... May he rest in peace! May God, in His judgment, which is so much milder and more compre-hending than our own, allow him infinite repose, in a world without the maturity and horror of this one.... At bottom, he was only a boy."*

Not much, one has to admit, in exchange for a normal Reader's patience, even if only in hope of simple entertainment.

Father De Biase—this is all we can offer, in embarrassment, since the report is so succinct and miserly, to satisfy a Reader's curiosity—had reached *I Portici* at two o'clock in the morning, at odds (after the message delivered by the servant) with what Giuliana and Rosanna had expected, and indeed (we presume) while the ladies were asleep; and he had immediately retired with Claus to the prince's studio. A light remained lit there for two hours. They spoke at length, the one as a Christian tutor, anxious to comfort and to offer aid, the other with the anguish of an ex-schoolboy who turned to the older man for the grace of reason—if not the reason of grace—in the face of the highest and yet disappointing readings on a question (he said) *of honor or supreme defeat.* The whole of human knowledge was passed in review, from Luther (the family's spiritual tradition had its roots in the Reformation) and the wandering Siddhartha Gautama, up to the terrible Nietzsche who had walked the streets of Turin—and the sublime Christian sword loomed over everything.... The whole of Nature had to be passed in review before the verdict could be reached: the whole of Nature, and its truest essence: the question as to whether or not, and with what knots, Nature was tied to man: and was she the very daughter of God, or had He instead forever damned and rejected her as wholly alien to everything divine? Saint Augustine too, as Rosanna's impassioned intelligence had supposed, was not left out of that debate—but Claus was to find him "superficial, and unacquainted," so he said "with the high gilded doors of Evil."

The baron was to learn at the end of it all that the happiness for which he hoped was impossible, that he was in error; and he saw his error to contain that sin for which there is no pardon, the sin of pride. And having been invited to retreat, *just barely in time,* (according to the Jesuit) from the edge of the abyss from which there is no return, having nearly been threatened as well (surely as a joke) that his ex-wife might be informed of the situation—and the news would have spread from her through all of New York—he seemed to accept the outcome with a disarming return to the air of calm and goodness which always before had most typified him. "I supposed him to be in some way deranged, if not truly ill," commented

Father De Biase, inclining his head, "and I imagined (perhaps too easily) that his final separation from Clara and the recent loss of his property in Sorrento were the immediate cause. How thoroughly I fooled myself!" He continued: "Claus went to the window, which was open on the black, sweet-smelling expanse of the gardens, and simply stood there. It framed not even the faintest light that wasn't supplied by the stars, and there wasn't so much as a single sound from anything other than the wayward night-time wind. He seemed to me to be highly relieved, or perhaps only resigned. And as he turned around, I was hoping our fearful question had been laid to rest. The hint of a smile on his grave and yet so open face, which showed all the purity of the beauty of the Asck... family, was the only message of peace he had to offer. But the words that came in its wake had nothing to do with that smile at all.

"'*He*, therefore,' the pronoun referring to God Himself, 'He, therefore,' in a high, penetrating voice, nearly as though we weren't in the middle of the night and there was no one whom he feared to wake, '*He* is truly of a nature that avoids perfection itself? Or doesn't He indeed abhor it? And that, good Father, can only mean that He did not consecrate His work—His Creation—to Perfection! I can only suppose that *He* wasn't even aware of so sublime a possibility.'

"'Be quiet, Claus, for love of your mother!' I said to him, 'poor woman, wherever she now abides, with her irrepressible hunger for freedom,' I thus avoided speaking of *sins*, 'for which you surely, with the pity of a son, have forgiven her....'

"'Yes, I have very strong feelings about my mother,' he replied, always rigid and calm, and nearly humble, but without ever lowering his overly powerful voice. 'But nothing is more important to me than the Perfection of

God's universe. If He Himself is anything else—and less than perfect—and through His church condemns the only feeling of absolute purity that links Humanity to the Source of all perfection—if He condemns the striving toward the Absolute and permits no more than life's funereal *norm*—where then can His pretended Perfection lie?'

"'Ah, be quiet, my unhappy boy,' I now cried out, no longer able to restrain myself, revealing the passion and the pain I felt at seeing him defeated and utterly, forever lost. I too forgot to lower my voice. 'Be quiet!' I cried. 'Can you truly imagine to find *perfection* in your marriage to an inferior creature! Can you call a servant the Source of the Universe? For this is what you seem to me to want to say!'

"That *hint of a smile*"—this is still the voice of Don Igino De Biase—"grew broader, and my embittered heart couldn't determine the attitude—was it irony or hostility?—with which he cried, in utter exaltation:

"'No! *She* is no inferior, father, and surely no servant! *She*, dear father, is the very mother of the Stars, and the Inspiration—in the realm beyond life *as it seems to us*—of the *first* God. She is therefore the mother and the sister of God, no servant at all.'

"'Not a servant? No? What else could she be?' I parried, in a tone of abhorrent dissent for which I will never forgive myself. 'So, please explain yourself....'

"'She is not a servant!' His face now streamed with tears. 'She is no poor creature chained to the moods of the Constellations, at least, father, not for me: she is my own very soul, my equal.... My peer in nobility and everything else...my eternal bride. And I intend this very morning to marry her, in Church, dressed in white.... And she'll wear that veil of Brussels lace which Clara never wore....'

"If he hadn't added these words, I wouldn't have

snapped to full wakefulness. But indeed he had wakened me entirely, and I shifted from the *tu* of the former professor to the *voi* of cold (and witless) social relations: 'Baron von Nebel,' I exclaimed, 'for the grace of God, return to yourself! Take hold of yourself!'"

A brief murmur of consternation arose and then quickly subsided among the Jesuit's listeners.

"Marriage! A church marriage! Dressed in white!"

"With a veil of Brussels lace.... In contempt, I imagine, of his first wife," one of the Reverend fathers murmured.

De Biase, while recalling his ordeal, had felt himself grow weak and distraught, but he made an effort to hide his commotion from those learned prelates.

"Nebel," he said, "almost immediately left the room. It was clear, moreover, to him as well as to me, that we had nothing more to say to one another. Shortly afterward, both hoping and fearing to find him waiting in the hallway, I too left the room.... The hallway was empty. The mysterious cold of daybreak flowed in through one of the high open windows."

At this point—with the clergyman's tale—we lose the only tenuous trace, as said before, of the rest of Nebel's story. And who his love, and what her name might have been—the impossible bride condemned by God—truly we will never know. In fact, the person who reported the conversation in Grenoble was later to contradict himself, and for a reason known to himself alone insisted that the city in which it took place was not Grenoble but Nîmes. Further investigation, at such a point, ceased to be worth the effort.

* * *

The tragic accident—if that is what it was, and not, as many were to think, at no great distance from our own conclusions, a true and proper suicide—took place about a half hour later. The high, elegant carriage that bore, at dawn—in flight—a guest from *I Portici*—in short, the carriage that carried Claus from the sublime Amalfi coast to the gay city of Naples from which he had arrived—plummeted from a curve of the gilded road that descends toward the *Dragone*, and there, on the dry streambed, it lay a shattered wreck. The German's proud brown head, entirely intact, but motionless, lay among the braces, the clear blue eyes still open, showing no fright, toward the May firmament, still flecked with stars on the one side, on the other veined with pink.

There rested on his breast, in confident abandon—so strangely after a plunge of six hundred feet, but along a fairly gentle decline—a long white face. And here, yes, were rivulets of diamonds...and still a light quiver of breath, a shiver, on its noble—perhaps a shiver of joy, perhaps of terror, one couldn't have said, but mainly, we believe, of peace—on its noble animal brow.

Where Time Is Another

At the beginning of the First World War—the period in which I was born—social discrepancies, in Italy as in many other parts of the world, were not, I believe, as painful as they are today. Above all, they were not so conspicuous. My family, a total of nine persons which included six children, lived a highly modest life, practically in poverty, in the south-central region of the country and was surely no stranger to economic hardship, but we didn't really notice it. At least the children didn't. So even in spite of having been born into very uncomfortable circumstances, often sad, and marked above all by a great void of culture and security, I wasn't aware of it, and perhaps didn't suffer from it, up until adolescence. And at that point, the center of my life came to be occupied by other problems, which quickly coalesced into a single problem: the problem of self-expression. The primary problem of survival—the universal problem, so to speak, which was to tarry at my side throughout the whole of my life—flanked this second and equally serious problem, making it sometimes more intricate, and at other times more simple. There were even moments when I managed to believe that self-expression was my only problem; but then I'd be forced to admit that the other problem remained as well. Both of them, now, like Poe's famous raven, have taken up permanent residence on the threshold of my life. My life has become their home.

But what is the nature of this problem of self-expression which can prove so strong as to vie with the problem of survival itself, and for all of a span, by now, of forty or fifty years? Today we are wary of discussing such things, since they don't seem sufficiently "democratic"—as the phrase currently runs. And yet if democracy is ever to prove its worth as the tool most suited for creating a certain happiness, I believe that the problem of self-expression—the problem of achieving a true individuality—may well have to occupy the very first place, and I mean within the lives of people in general.

Self-expression: a child most usually achieves self-expression by drawing, playing, fantasizing, and running, and even by inventing another "I" which offers protection from the world. Adolescents are apt to turn their attention to the ins and outs of much more sophisticated techniques, desiring to translate the act of self-expression into the production of something concrete they can call their own. If such adolescents have been blessed with adequate education, their efforts will be crowned with success, and the creative "I" will experience harmonious growth. But this period in which the adolescent wants to give autonomous form (autonomous and therefore new) to what she or he feels, is highly delicate, and things can go quite wrong. The world can overwhelm such a boy or girl with its own cultural models; or models may prove to be wholly lacking, as is typically the pitfall in highly impoverished societies. The adolescent runs the risk, in the first case, of being brainwashed and enslaved; or, in the second, of being set adrift into a course of distorted development. The present-day world of childhood and adolescence is full of such boys and girls—captive to society's values in the wealthy countries, and abandoned to their own devices in the poor ones.

To dwell at greater length on this situation would not be easy, not now. But if I want to reach some personal understanding of the mystery that drives the curious destiny of a certain kind of writer—the writer who comes from nowhere, and then returns into nowhere without having achieved what he or she desired to achieve, even in spite of having dedicated a large part of his or her life to this precious enterprise—I have to remain aware of the *gravity* of this situation: the situation of the adolescent who searches for a means of self-expression by way of education—a means of self-expression and thus a means of growth—but who cannot find it. Because education is itself impossible and unavailable. Because the one specific world in which he or she lives has no such thing to offer. Such young people are thus thrown back on their own resources: they don't give up the struggle (it's a battle for survival no less than for self-expression), but their achievements never fulfill their potential. Not by far. And finally—at the end of a life—they have to accept the perception that circumstance has shown more muscle than their own determination, and has greatly hampered their capacity for self-expression, and their growth as well. That's what I want to talk about. But first, before proceeding, I have to return for a moment to what I understood at fifteen years of age—and still today understand—by "self-expression," which centers, for me, on the written word.

I don't want to dwell on any deeply personal view—or, worse, on any self-satisfied interpretation—of the meaning of self-expression. So I do better to focus on self-expression in terms of its value as a mode of "intelligence," rather than as linked to the life of the feelings; I do better to confront its concern with the *logic* of things, and to skirt the vanity of finding oneself, like a mirror, in the midst of them. I have used the word *things*. And as a curious faculty peruses and presents us with things in their countless number, manifest variety and endless mutability, this word fills up, little by little, with a special air or meaning. Its meaning is involved—as far as I myself am concerned, or as far as my experience can fathom—with what I'd refer to as "strangeness." And there you have it. If I had to offer a definition of everything that surrounds me—things, in their infinitude, and the feelings through which I grasp them, by now throughout half a century—I could hinge it on no other word: strangeness. My writings reflect the desire—indeed the painful urgency—to render this feeling of strangeness.

For adults—or among highly cultivated peoples—the whole world is the world of the obvious, of the commonplace. They apply their labels to everything—pricing and, whenever need be, describing the merchandise. This is a *field*, this is the *ocean*, this is a *horse*, this is your *mother*, this is the *national flag*, these are two *boys*. But for children, or adolescents, and for a certain sort of artist as well—less often for writers—that's not the way things stand. Wherever they go, everything shines with a light that betrays no origins. Everything they touch—that flag, that horse, that ocean—is vibrant with electricity and leaves them wonderstruck. They understand what adults have ceased to understand: that the world *is a heavenly body*; that all things within and beyond the world are made of cosmic matter; and that their nature, their meaning—except for a dazzling gentleness—is unsoundable. Children are moved to tears by everything they touch or see pass by, and they vainly appeal to reason or their elders for explanations of the why and how of so much magnificence: those elders (including parents and teachers) are usually no more informed and attentive than so many inkwells. The child is alone. And the child's approach and descent to the earth and the so-called real-life world is often, finally, a collision. A moment of impact and ecstasy. The possession of a means of self-expression—a means of self-expression and an education in its use—might mean at such an instant to find oneself provided with a cushion or a parachute. It might bring the ability to engage with the world—the world of reality—in the way that's right and proper for the human soul: through the exercise of creativity. Otherwise, when children connect to the outside world solely by way of the objects supplied by the marketplace, they remain exposed to an inward anxiety; in spite of possessing everything, they experience an internal void that turns frequently into bitter dissatisfaction, and anger. Because their education, their birth into the world, took place without the aid of their own creativity and sense of invention. Such a child finds everything already made. And the already made—by others—will be found to be utterly destructive, like a faceless wall. So it's something that the child in turn will want to destroy, once having seen it to stand in the service of imaginative and creative amputation. I have always thought that the world's greatest problem—the problem on which its peace as well, no matter how relative, may very well depend—is to allow its children to enter the so-called adult world as persons who themselves *create*, rather than appropriate and destroy. Creativity is a form of motherhood. It educates; it makes us happy; it makes adulthood something positive. Not to create is to die; and before dying, to grow irremediably old.

Such pure if difficult happiness is often found among children who live—without great strain—in poor communities, but surrounded by fundamentally loving people. They escape the immediate embrace of the feeling that the essence of human community lies in profit and loss. Such notions remain at a distance from their souls, and they are meanwhile able to live though days that are charged with joy and meaning; for a good stretch of time they swim outside the sway of the currents that end in the whirlpool of economic conditioning, escaping all false social obeisance to the things and interests of the marketplace. They'll encounter these violent forces at fifteen or sixteen years of age, when already they'll have sufficient strength; and not everything within them will come away shattered or damaged.

I had five brothers, and none of them, it seems to me, showed any particular inclination to the arts. But one of them—he went to a naval academy and then died in the war—wrote a very beautiful, very limpid story when he was twenty years old; its subject was a smuggler who had been arrested. He also wrote a poem on the mysteries of the stars. Another of my brothers—already an adult, and quite unhappy—turned to painting for a number of years and worked in bright, glowing colors. When a psychological crisis led him to set this activity aside, he became unhappy once again. Concerning my other brothers, I remain largely in the dark, since they were scattered here and there by the war and rarely—those who survived—came back home. But traces of a kind of nostalgia for a state of youthful creativity remain to be seen in several of them, and it strikes me that this need, if only they had developed it in time, along with the rest of the faculties that belong to living in the world and understanding it, might have changed their lives.

Even if my own life isn't what one thinks of as a totally realized life, I have to think of myself as fortunate; because I have sometimes managed, in the course of at least some fifty years of adult life, to reach the luminous shore—I think of myself as eternally shipwrecked—of a form of self-expression and creativity that find their never swerving goal in the hope of capturing and fixing—if only for an instant, meaning the span of time encompassed by a work of art—the marvelous phenomenon of living and feeling.

And there's nothing romantic, and no self-indulgence, in my use of the word "marvelous." Of all the words that might be employed as descriptions of life and the feeling of being alive, "marvelous" is surely the most pedestrian word I know. This feeling is better approached by words like "ecstasy," by terms like "ecstatic," "fugitive," "inscrutable."

My first such emotions were aroused by the evanescent beauty of the face of a child who lived next-door to us. I was struck by the purity and chestnut sweetness of his gaze. A "phenomenon." Of that much I was sure. But how could I render it? A few pastels came to my aid. And if I saw, having hidden the drawing in a closet, that a person who absentmindedly opened the closet door betrayed a moment of surprise and an inkling of having been moved, I understood that I had reached my goal of grasping and expressing the flow of life. I drew and drew, like so many adolescents, but only faces: mysterious, childlike faces. Confronted with something that spoke of adulthood, I could draw—I could capture—nothing. The emotion set off in me by very young faces was not of course the only emotion I encountered: all the phenomena of nature—principally the wind—struck me as fluid, unsoundable *faces* of the power of nature. Flowers as well, naturally enough, and grasses, the sun, Sunday mornings, the lunar nights with many clouds that pass before the moon. Or little shards of glass that sparkled on the ground in some gloomy, silent street. Everything struck me as containing a warning and a message. Such things were more intense and secret than feelings, and they couldn't be rendered—at least I couldn't render them—with pastels. So I had to turn to the pen. But that pen was completely unpracticed. My intellect—though at most I should say my sensibility—hadn't at all been schooled to the use of writing. I hadn't been educated. As with many girls of the time, my education had come to a close with elementary school. So from adolescence until about the age of twenty—the period in which I first encountered this problem of expressing myself through writing—I never indulged the illusion that I might be able to solve it. But I constantly circled around it, and I did learn something.

I had left school when I was just about thirteen—after a woeful experience at an institute for vocational training—and my family had afterwards given in to my request to enroll me at a private school for the piano. It was run by a relative. The plan was for me to earn a diploma, to pass the examinations at the conservatory, and then to find pupils to whom I myself could give private lessons. These studies continued for three or four years—I studied music, a fact that still surprises me—and then I broke it all off quite abruptly. Another terrible passion, a terrible event, had found its way into my stock of experience, and there was no way at all to give it expression through those sheets of music. It's an event that merits brief mention.

In addition to all the unsoundable faces and events that daily erupt from life—these things I ardently desired to capture and fix in all their beauty and evanescence—I had also come to understand that life is charged with a number of cadences, or properties, of which the nature is equally unsoundable. One of them, for example, lay in the immensity, somnolence, and peacefulness of space. I had had that experience in Libya, between nine and thirteen years of age, perhaps: the way nature, as sand or sky, knows the immobility and endless extent, within immobility, of dream. Then, while crossing the sea to return to Italy—a two day voyage—I was struck quite intensely by the duplex motion which derived, on the one hand, from the ship that cut its way through the dark blue waters, and, on the other, from the waters themselves: they were never the *same* blue waters of only a moment before, but still they presented themselves as such. So the same place, I thought, doesn't mean an identical time and situation. This doubly articulated mechanism—the workings of life and place inside the mechanics of time—cast a shadow across my path. The ship was moving and kept on moving while I stood still and observed the very same sea, and meanwhile the ship's situation had changed: it lay in another but apparently identical place. And the place it had been in before—yesterday's place—had irretrievably disappeared. So, the problem was time itself: the problem of the places and dimensions *into which things passed.* The very fact that *things passed!* And once and for all, it seemed. So, from a logical point of view, *everything that happened*—if its second, ulterior state lay in its existing no longer—was necessarily illusory. This quality of time, its practice of forming things and then of canceling them out, acted profoundly on my mind, no less than those forms themselves. I saw it all as a great enigma. Time consumed itself; and what happened to the forms in which every moment of time gave proof of itself?

One of these forms—to return to the fact that prevented my continuing to study music—was one of my brothers, whom to tell the truth I didn't know well. He too hadn't wanted or been able to study, and for the last two years he had been at sea as a crewman on some ship. Now, one January evening, we received the news that he was dead—in a distant place, on the shores of a distant sea—and would never again return to Naples and the life we lived as a family.

At first this piece of news turned our house into a place of infernal turmoil, which later, however, gave way to a strange silence. Such silence always follows a death, even the deaths of pets, and it strikes me as resulting from a kind of collapse of the soul. Something has been amputated. A part of the soul has taken its leave forever. And the soul reacts by entirely ceasing to listen to the noises, sounds and voices of surrounding nature, no less than to its own. This silence, I believe, is of the very same nature as the great and distant azure of the vault of African skies—or of the skies of other vast continents—and it holds the same mute rumble of the sea that falls away behind a ship. So, beyond its azure vault—its happy soul—these are the world's most patent events: time—the eternal flow and vanishing of everything; and this is the response of nature and the soul: the sudden voicelessness, the stricken creature's collapse into itself. So there's a very great truth in Dante's depiction of a soul suddenly wounded and deprived of a part of itself: he tells us that Calvalcanti, believing his son to be dead, cried out "What? What did you say? He had had? Does he live no longer?" and then collapsed into the burning arc, never to reappear again.

This silence, at least for me, in my never ending solitude (my mother could look for succor in her Christian faith, my brothers had school, my father had his office) lasted for several months, and I saw no way of getting out of it. Finally one day, indeed one morning, suddenly, I thought that—if nothing else, since it was killing me—

I could describe it. So I sat down at my table and wrote a free-verse poem of about a hundred lines, titled *Manuele*, in which I talked about this silence to the sailor's ghost. That was my first poem. And since I wasn't—later—to write very many poems, but mostly stories, it also counts as my first attempt at writing: my first attempt to couple the written word to a calm frame of mind and to use it to render—aesthetically to render—something atrocious, and above all else inscrutable. Life is an apocalyptic phenomenon—apocalyptic and beguiling; and it is so intense and so averse to every form of examination or analysis, from no matter what point of view—it counts as no less than a synonym for the unsoundable and ungraspable—that it can only be rendered by a contrary frame of mind: by an attitude of admiration, by a contemplation of its very immensity, and of what for us is its ferocity. Affliction requires that we take up a musical instrument—in this case verse—and attempt to sound a first few calm and smiling notes: it's only within that calm, and by means of that smile, that we'll be able to imprison the horror we have suffered. Think, for example, of a mirror. That cold, elegant and utterly motionless surface can capture the shudders of a wind-blown tree, or a great green beast of a wave as it rises up to scud along the surface of the sea. No sea could reflect the sea, nor a tree a tree. The nature and the tragic spirit of things can only be reflected in something of an utterly different, contrasting nature. In something endowed with what we refer to as aesthetic quality. The quality of the mirror, which stands in opposition to what it reflects, and is therefore able to encompass it. If you want to capture a stormy sea, or the horrors of a war, stay calm; your own pained silence is charged with a distance, and you must place that distance between these things and yourself.

* * *

These thoughts arise on their own, and surely in disorder, but I have no other way of turning a personal and therefore limited experience into something universal, and therefore clear to everyone. The fact that it's a part of my personal history would itself be of no importance if it weren't accessible to others.

After writing these verses—a total of three poems—I decided to send them to a literary magazine which I had often noticed at the kiosk not far from our house. (This experience too—submitting the results of one's first uncertain attempts at self-expression to the judgment of a learned authority—is both inevitable and educational.) Then I waited for a reply. And here I was lucky. Because the person who received and opened my letter—the director of the magazine—was a spirit of superior elevation. In other words, he was one of the deacons of the great Temple of Aesthetics, and he knew it to be the forge in which the human soul assumes its proper shape. He felt a very great love for the human soul, but like the saints and great theologians he never saw its growth and salvation as divorced from the observance of religious Law and Rule. He saw faith and obedience to the great tables of Aesthetic Law as fundamental. This was the only route through which the human soul could find salvation. He published this long piece of writing (I won't dwell on my joy, I had known no equal joy) and offered me as well a few suggestions; but his comments were always so detached and apparently marginal as to stay at a distance from both praise and disfavor (and at the time I was largely unaware even of the use of the apostrophe). His discretion has always made me think of him as a true educator.

My life, from that day forward, changed radically, since now I had an instrument with which to express myself. I also had something to which to aspire, a compelling goal: the approval of my invisible teacher. I spent about a year on this kind of work: setting all the commotion which life aroused within me into free hendecasyllabic verse, and seeing it grow instantly calm and turn into something *different* (a formal feeling). The experience was full of joy and liberation, even if the poems themselves were nothing special. But I was training my hand, teaching my fingertips to write, and in my boundless nothingness as a girl who had no future, this also, if not quite simply, seemed to hold the offer—I dare to say—of a place in society.

At this point, the editor of the literary magazine (which was printed in a far-away city) asked me to try to write a story—a story in prose—for a weekly publication with which he was also connected. This was my entrance examination to the much-loved school of writing (no matter how laxly I may have followed its courses). I immediately wrote the story "Redskin," and he published it, accompanied by a few words of praise, calling no attention to its defects.

I'd run the risk of going astray in numberless rivulets of narrative, of memory and observation, if I didn't stick strictly to the facts. My promotion (quite the proper term) to literature, or at least to its introductory courses, also earned me a higher level of respect at home, and surely I couldn't ignore the salutary change that took place in my mother as she dwelt on the thought that perhaps her difficult daughter was acquiring a profession. This was also the period in which the director of the magazine introduced me—in French, a language I had studied a bit, alone, but which in any case I understood—to two of the stories of Katherine Mansfield: "Prelude" and "On the Bay." I found myself to be looking up at peaks that shone in the sun. Such beauty was wholly new to me. I'm not quite certain if he introduced me to the work of Katherine Mansfield because of first having read a lengthy story of my own—"The Solitary Light"—or if instead I wrote "The Solitary Light" in the wake of having read these stories. Aside from Katherine Mansfield's greatness, and from all her fully accomplished art, there's a certain similarity between these two ways of seeing things—on the part, on the one hand, of Katherine Mansfield, and on the other hand, of that nameless girl: a gilded atmosphere, uncertainties that might belong to dreams, a sense of ineffability, of the tender inexplicability of things...and as well, I'd add, of the soul's befuddlement and constant trembling and loss of itself. As far as everything else is concerned, the difference was enormous and has never ceased to be: in terms not only of aesthetic results—on her part deservedly famous, on my part no more than uncertain—but also as a question of the very nature of the experiences involved. Mansfield belonged quite clearly to a cultured, bourgeois society, highly developed and pan-European, and she was able to connect interior experience to the worlds of physical and social reality; whereas for me the worlds of physical and social reality remained entirely unknown. I couldn't avoid the sad realization, bit by bit as I tried to move ahead, that I found it ever less possible to recognize things for what they truly were and to call them by their proper names: my intelligence, since it hadn't been equipped with the arms of knowledge and factuality, withdrew into the merely contemplative, the emotive, to the point of going astray. So a certain sense of the coldness of life became my only world, and expressing it my only goal: a goal already outstripped by the narrative canons of the past, and with me they therefore took on an air of weary repetition.

These words refer to all of my stories of the period

before the war, and as well to a few that were written later—the stories that went into the volumes which appeared in 1937 and 1948, entitled *Angelici dolori* and *Infanta Sepolta*. All of these thirty or so stories, including the ones I didn't publish, were attempts—at first quite happy, but then ever more neurotic and tortured—to render my sense of ecstasy and wonder on first encountering the world, and then the distress of seeing this world turn ever more into a desert where nothing seemed to hold a meaning or move towards any destination: a world of ghosts and monsters. And the first of these ghosts was that little girl who had made those observations on the ship and the area *of yesterday* into which that ship had to pass. This child was instinctively devoted to musing and contemplation, and to taking possession of ever more rare and singular emotions; and this world already withered by war, this world in which the civilization of the eighteenth and nineteenth centuries no longer existed, and where a new and very sinister civilization was coming to the fore, had truly ceased to hold a place for her. Even more than in her narrative style, her desperation is clearly seen in the subjects to which she turned her attention: gracious spirits, solitary youths, God himself—in the guise of a handsome young man, but rather lifeless; or again in the places of which she wrote: places outside of time, poorly illuminated streets, abandoned gardens, prisons, deserts. Much as in De Chirico's universe (though I wasn't to meet De Chirico until a somewhat later date) or among the French Surrealists, the world was no longer inhabited, and everything concerned with the human being had already turned into memory and regret. The whole of livable time, in my first bizarre stories, was something that belonged to the past—even while remaining present—and was seen from a place outside of it. The chance to live within it would never occur again.

* * *

If one stops to consider that these stories were the whole of my *reality* on the eve of the war, throughout those four long years, and afterwards as well, one will see how hostile my mind had become—"hostile" is the word I have to use—to what one currently refers to as existential experience, or the actual world. I rejected it simply *by saying nothing about it*. Of this there can be no doubt.

So, the tragedy of my life (a euphoric expression, so ingenuous as nearly to amuse me, since life is always tragic, even the lives of a blade of grass or a single atom, and nothing truly escapes this tragic dimension, which lies in being "swept along," irresistibly) lay in my almost immediate discovery that everything—even people, faces, books—was only void and appearance: *images*, of which the freedom and material substance were totally illusory. A single thing was truly alive, and nearly counted as separate and distinct from the life of matter: pain and painful emotion (which I also understand to include love and joy). So I quickly discovered that I had to do battle for something—for life—which in fact was an abyss and a sense of hopeless loss. I was very much aware of that, but this awareness didn't relieve me of my task. Writing was my battle; and my instrument for writing, for the constant task of fixing the fluid and ecstatic, consisted of an idiom that can only be described as *infantile*, when compared to the regular arms of even an ordinary writer My vocabulary was quite restricted; my knowledge of grammar and syntax almost rudimentary. My acquaintance with genius and the masters of the written word was limited to only a very few—poets, like Poe—whom I had encountered at used book stalls. A desperate undertaking; and yet I had no choice: if I didn't write, I could only return into nothingness.

These were the years just before the war. And it was

now that I opened my eyes and saw the true conditions in which my family lived: a wretched house, dilapidated furniture, debts. That, sadly, was the truth of the matter. And soon, since I hadn't studied or learned a trade, I could only look forward, at the age of twenty-two or twenty-three, to finding myself in the streets.

So it came as a great relief—no matter how surprised I was, and no matter how much it felt like stealing—to receive a proposal for the publication of all of my first stories in a single collected volume: a proposal from Massimo Bontempelli, the writer who had succeeded my first patron as the editor of the literary magazine. I accepted, and it all came about immediately. I myself had nothing to do with it (at the time there weren't a great many people who wrote) and I also received a prize, in money—five thousand Lire—with which I could help my father to bring a bit of order, at least momentarily, into our household's disastrous finances.

My recall of these days and occurrences, now so remote, isn't sufficiently clear to allow me say if I was finally happy. But I don't think I had enough time. Events ran one right after another, just as the cars of a train follow the ones before them, now in a tunnel, now out in the open light. But the stretches of open light were ever more brief, fleeting, finished in a flash. Then suddenly the start of an endless darkness. The war. That's the way I remember the war.

Our house was destroyed during one of the very first bombings, and I found myself, in the course of those four or five years, with a mutilated family (brothers dead, or missing, or prisoners of war) as we wandered all throughout Italy, all the way to the Veneto, where we lived on the island of Burano. Before the war—a year or two before it began—I had already spent a year in Venice, working as a proofreader for a newspaper. The war turned my thoughts to Burano as a place without bombs. After our house in the district of Naples' port had fallen—a rented house, and already decrepit on its own account—it struck me as sensible to take my parents and other relatives there. We lived—part of us—in the house of the village street cleaner, but the place was safer and more amenable than anywhere in Lazio, where, as I later learned, true horror was taking place.

And this word: *horror.* My experience, up until that time, may indeed have prevented me from seeing its meaning in anything other than social or historical terms, but still it was the last great word I learned to apply to the universal framework in which we live our lives.

Space; *azure skies*; *dream*; then *time* (yesterday's absence, the shifting position of the human ship); then the sudden disappearances of human beings; then *silence*. And now, finally, *horror*: those recurrent periods of generalized slaughter—folk against folk, man against man—that then unfailingly find their termination in a peace in which the only thing no longer possible is justice for the dead, which is to speak of their resurrection.

In a short span of time—that's what fifteen years amount to within the space of a life—I had made the acquaintance of almost everything that defines our existence as human beings: the beatitude and impossibility of seeing it endure; wonder and the struggle to express it; the majesty of fully achieved expression and the immaterial greatness of literature; and the gulf that divides them from *explanation*, and from all our daily confusions. *Over there*, every beatitude—but like the light of a star already exploded. Over here, the miserable frenzy of the fall which has already happened, of existence as the already devastated dream.

All that remained was life itself—no longer any literature—and what a life!

I was ever more repulsed by reality—the mortal spoils, rather than the essence of the real—and my desire to find refuge in words was ever more intense and ever more desperate. But writing demanded conditions—a minimum of economic security—which had nothing to do with my own.

On returning to Naples in 1945, I found myself in precisely the future I had once foreseen. I was homeless. The generosity of a few friends kept me going (otherwise I wouldn't now be alive and able to write these memoirs) but only when the going was roughest. I see myself for example as I hunted for a furnished room, recoiling at its gloom and the roaches; or while making an evening meal of a couple of doughnuts and a glass of wine, thanks to contributions from a couple of friends; or sitting in the kitchen of a well-to-do family, once they had finished lunch, consuming the plate of food they had set aside for me. I see myself in pawn shops, relieving myself of a typewriter or other personal objects. Or in the streets of old Naples, on a morning lit by a melancholy sun, as I bargain with a vendor for a new typewriter ribbon, for a portable: a session of bargaining that ended in a brawl. Or I am sweeping out an office (the seat of some sort of political organization, of which the time knew so many) and taking excited exception to quite legitimate observations on the dust I hadn't removed. Or I am here and there throughout the city climbing endless stairs, trying to make a living as a bill collector. Then, suddenly, I'm getting onto trains for Milan, for Reggio Calabria, for Rome. Or I'm all in a desperate tither while boarding the packet boat for Palermo; I remember the kindly face of the unknown captain, and the help he was good enough to give me.

All of that lasted for five or six years, and now remains in my memory as a kind of inferno, but I don't really know if it was, since I was very strong. This was also the period, even while continuing from time to time to write a tale or two, in which I turned my attention to journalism. Again I had a bit of luck. A few of my longer, and I think more attentive, pieces on the city of Naples earned me the attention of Luigi Einaudi, who was then the President of the Republic, and he came to my assistance in a great many ways: with money, by supplying me with train tickets, and above all by arranging for the Olivetti Corporation to invite me to live as their guest in Ivrea for two or three months. It was there that I completed nearly all of the final work on my third book: *Il mare non bagna Napoli*, which dealt with precisely this subject, with the conditions of life in southern Italy in the period after the war—conditions which made themselves apparent in the postwar period, but which came in fact from a long way back: no less (according to me) than from a tradition of Nature worship, which I attributed to the people of Naples.

How ingenuous. I now reject this thesis, or at least any need to talk about it. Never again, today, would I affirm that Nature in any way harms us. I simply accept the perception that life at the level of nature—like the lives of domestic animals—is impossible for the human being; and that any attempt to adopt such a form of life—as in part it was adopted in Naples, and partly inculcated by an unreformed church—will lead to our certain undoing. Yet even if this book was grounded on a faulty thesis, it nonetheless had said something new, revealing an Italy that stood deprived of that spirit of charity or mutual assistance which truly forms the basis of civilized life and its institutions; and since at the time we weren't so sensitive to flaws and shortcomings, it enjoyed quite favorable reception. And I suddenly—living alone in Milan, my family a thing of the past—I suddenly found myself (as the saying goes) almost famous. Famous, but still with no money, since books didn't get sold in large numbers of copies. This book sold something like seven or eight thousand copies, but I had already asked for several advances and nothing more was due to me. So I had to continue to make do as best I could. There was still no question, for quite some time, of being able to set up a home of my own, and I continued to live in furnished rooms. And when I finally took an apartment—taking on as well a rent contract—I was quick to lose it: my sporadic earnings couldn't cover all the bills.

This was the point when my mind began to dwell on another of the sadder sides of human life; I began to grasp the gravity of owning nothing while living in the midst of a system based on the privileges of property. I began to grasp the way life slowly falls apart in the effort to please or satisfy the proprietors—including the owners of newspapers—always painting a pleasant picture of their systems. There was no possible meeting ground, no possible comparison between these squalid, beautiless exercises and true writing, true Self-Expression, which seemed to me to embody the freedom, the absolute freedom, of the human mind. For a moment I had fondly imagined that writing conferred the right to write again, but now I saw that this *again*, if writing didn't turn into a source of money, was destined to decorate the banner of still another fond Illusion. Courage, in a certain sense, abandoned me. I was like a badly injured soldier who then had found bandages with which to dress his wounds; but then they wound him again; and now he can find no other bandages, and dies from loss of blood.

I was doing advertising. And between one job and another, for this or that product, I wrote a series of melancholy "pieces" (melancholy and without great vigor, as I now remember them) on the real conditions of life in Milan, as seen through my immigrant's eyes. I saw a city where everything was for sale, where everything was decked with a price tag, and where the tasks of art and writing—the contemplation and definition of the world—enjoyed no further hopes. Art and writing lay crushed beneath the weight of foreign fashions that found their strength, quite precisely, in the vision they offered of vast, foreign markets. I thus became aware of what it can mean for a nation to find itself mortgaged to the great cosmopolitan markets and to have no further space or freedom in which to pursue a road of its own. Too many concessions to money—when the problem of survival appears to be the only one, presenting itself, moreover, not only as a question of survival, but also of successful competition with the keener survival techniques of more prosperous peoples—mean the loss of all hope for those who find their work in the field of self-expression. The field narrows down to masquerades and conformity.

I had nothing that was any longer salable, other than clichéd slogans. In as early as 1960, freedom of expression in Italy was only apparent, and in fact a thing of the past. The actual life of the country already lay in the hands of the mass media, which daily undermined it and made it incapable of understanding language—that language of "symbol" which in fact is the language that literature speaks. Symbol was the language in which I spoke, and no one any longer could direct attention to a thing like that. Attention waned, and the market vanished.

Just before leaving Milan—a step I had finally understood I had to take—I dashed off a story, in the space of a month, which was intended as sarcastic and amusing, but which turned out instead to be quite delicate. *Il Cappello piumato*. I never saw it as a full-fledged book, but there were ways in which it was dear to me. It was only some twenty years later that I managed to see it published. At a time when people could see it, somehow or another, as making a political statement. The political—close on the heels of the vapid and salacious—is nowadays, here in Italy, the surest route to acceptability. And perhaps that's somewhat unfortunate.

The 1960s were already underway. I moved to Rome and wrote a brief novel, entitled *L'Iguana*. A book that was charged with scorn and rebellion. Rebellion in its style, since I suddenly abandoned all superficial realism; and scorn in its pretended equanimity in the face of human folly, and of the folly of the notion of class. A gentleman travels to an island—he's very rich and can go wherever he pleases—where he makes the acquaintance of a monster. He accepts it as something quite possible, and would like to effect its reintegration—presuming it to have suffered some sort of a *fall*—into human, or indeed bourgeois society, which he sees as the summit of virtue. But he has made a mistake: this monster is truly a monster, and indeed discloses the soul, at its purest and profoundest, of the Universe—of which the gentleman has lost all knowledge, if not for the knowledge that it's merchandise, that all of it can be given a price tag, that stars can be leased and bought and sold, and so on and so forth. The story didn't come to a happy ending (it concluded with Nature in a state of revolt), and after a bit of thought I changed it, adding another which was lighter and more serene, thinking that this might save the book from disparaging remarks on the part of silly critics, and thus might give it a chance on the market. But it didn't sell in any case. One thousand nine hundred and ninety copies in five years hardly amounts to a book's having sold.

Another regrettable aspect (though surely it has its justifications) of the economics of publishing—aside from the huge promotion campaigns set up for the marketing of vacuum-cleaner books—is the use that publishers make of books, without any need to ask anyone's approval, when once it's established (when they have established) that it's difficult to sell them. Such books can get passed on, *en bloc*, to various clubs and remainderers, with a truly risible percentage for the author. You then know nothing more about that book. Maybe you receive a check for sixteen thousand and fifty Lire in *rights* for a whole year. In short, the book—often well known and in demand—ends up, with no further involvement of the author, as an object of private exchange between two or three or any number of publishing companies. It travels a road of its own, of which it's presumed that the author has no need to know the various stations, or markets. You could say that the author can't so much as send an occasional postcard to his or her creature. The book by now is the property of a business concern (the publishing house) that can use it as it best sees fit, for the whole of a lifetime, employing it for any purpose at all, or otherwise for simple retransformation into kitchen rags—by pulping it.

There were so many things I had understood, and so many things that no longer made any difference to me. Once the *Iguana* was over and done with—it's still in circulation and still gets sold, but brings me no hint of money, thanks to the former receipt of a few advances—I returned to Milan and wrote an ironic little book: the irony lay in the schoolboy style I used for narrating sad and insignificant events. I had lost all belief in the printed page! *Poveri e semplici*. But the book was very easy reading, and therefore did fairly well, for a couple of years, even winning a prize; and I have to admit I have never forgotten it, even if it's not a book in which I recognize myself. Perhaps there was something good in it. I imagined that it might perhaps have given me a little money and made my life a little easier; that it might have offered me a little stability, and above all a house: this, by now, was my only dream. But that's not the way it worked out. Once again I had to return the advances received from the publisher in the course of several years (including the advances for two other books of stories which had found no market at all) and quite soon I again found myself staring into the face of slim probabilities of physical survival.

This was the moment—towards the end of 1960s—when another publishing company, of imposing proportions, sailed up to the flanks of the small, tarred, and much-patched hull of my old Florentine publisher, clearly intent on boarding maneuvers. I myself, it seemed, was the booty they had in mind. And a part of me was already willing to make its peace with the notion of leaving Florence—or what Florence meant in the publishing world, with its grace and good form, as a place where culture was still untouched by mammoth business interests, a place that still consisted *only* of culture, but tremendously poor—in favor of Milan. For money! I felt an enormous need for rest, that was the whole of it, for a place where money might be found: a place that offered a truce, by means of money, to the body and the weary soul. I imagined that the moment had come to get busy—strange isn't it?—so as finally to be able to *rest*. I fondly believed that this sort of rest was permitted to *all* writers, which is not at all the way things stood. The law demands—it is nothing less than a law, and a highly mysterious law—that precisely the weariest never find repose, and that the battle cry of life resound unceasingly around their heads. "Stunned," wrote Coleridge, "by that loud and dreadful sound."

This was the state of mind—stunned by dint of living in an endless hell of emotions, reactions and images that uninterruptedly followed one another, and also needful of a means of survival—in which I readied myself, in March 1969, to write my most recent book, *Porto di Toledo.*

My plan with *Porto di Toledo*, initially, was to write a free and happy "introduction" to my early stories, the stories in *Angelici dolori*, which I had been planning to suggest that my publisher in Florence reissue. But the question of where and with whom to publish the book rapidly ceased to interest to me, and my mind turned entirely to the narrative experiment itself: the experiment of reproposing a former world—the *old*—while mixing it with the *new*, which instantly bathed it in a different light, and subjected it to commentary. The *old* consisted of a few of the stories and poems I had written during the period of the literary magazine. As little by little I reached an understanding of the relationship between *life and expressive dream* which at the time had lain beneath them, I recalled and wrote about the real events of the period in which I had thought them up. And it's clear that this commentary held very little "criticism." Whatever might appear to be a criticism of my own work was simply *a new imaginative event.* (I seem, in fact, to have no doubt that all true criticism, of art as of the world, has to take up a place on the outside, and never on the inside, or as an act of participation.) So, to say that I was "criticizing" or writing a commentary on my expressive efforts of the 1930s amounts to nothing more than a turn of phrase. Rather than criticize, I was only involved in *reliving* that time of hopeless shipwreck (so hopeless, perhaps, as even to have held no desperation) and my appeal to abstract judgment was only a way of pulling it back more clearly into view. (Rather than to any true judgment, I appealed to a *figure* of judgment, which in fact opened out into an act of ulterior participation.) This *second part* of the book—this second part which embraces and winds in and out among the older writings—was therefore the *real book*, and I can add that affection and disgust for that period of time and the special way in which I then expressed myself (in the 1930s) were nearly all that *Toledo* hoped to formulate.

This plan, from my own point of view, was quite clear, and I'm certain that proper surroundings would have led to achieving the results I was aiming for. I could have counted on finding fluency by flowing ineffably back and forth through memories of writing and the life attached to it. But the actual surroundings in which I was living at the time—1969 and the following years—unleashed a level of aggravation that affected not only my former mode of expression—in yesterday's stories and poems—but equally the mode of expression I was working with today, which is to speak of my *oppressed and enchanted* reappraisal of those former times. The whole of *Toledo*, half-way through it, turned into something else: I ceased to be in control of the operation.

What surfaced now into the midst of my life—the life of a writer who lives in obscurity, or without the mothering protection of a provident and benevolent society, knows so many reversals!—was simply a question of noise. In this moment of fatigued disaffection for the outside world, I was living in Milan, in Via Mulino delle Armi. The room I used as my studio, the sort of studio I had always had, measured no more than a few square meters, and air passed freely through its narrow window (barely sixteen inches wide) only in the winter. Toward March, when I started to write, and well into April, this little window was always open, and sufficient air indeed flowed through it. But after the middle of April (I was then beginning the book's second section, "Terra in lutto," and the parts that follow) it had to stay shut, since all sorts of work were being done in the streets, and the building was also being renovated. Suffocation, and the nightmare was underway. I got up early, but that wasn't enough. I tightened a scarf around my head (around my ears); again that wasn't enough. This noise lay always at the edge of my thoughts, and as soon as it began, at eight o'clock in the morning, something inside of me snapped: my equilibrium snapped. That mirror I have spoken of was shattered. Unable to write, I only made notes. I said to myself, I'll write later on, while working on the second draft. And that was the way—quivering with mental pain—in which I wrote that ghostly, unstable, stuttered and highly repetitive part of *Toledo* called "Terra in lutto." That was the way I wrote it, since no other way was open to me. And I saw that the rhythm—in the shift from the first to the second section—wasn't at all what I had planned on. Some sort of suture had remained unsealed. The second part of the book seemed displaced, I'd say, by several meters from the first; and it clearly revealed that here we were sailing on another boat: this was no comment on life as experienced yesterday: it was life as lived right now, with all its suffocation and delirium.

The second part of my memories of *Toledo* thus seemed to be compromised, but I didn't despair of being able to save it—if various conditions could be brought to bear on the second draft at the typewriter.

That was the only goal of the life I was living then (a life, moreover, that knew no consolations) and still today I am able to imagine that I might have reached it, if destiny—my personal destiny, which I no longer guide, accepting instead that it guides me—hadn't arranged things differently.

I had to move—the reasons are already clear—and I moved from Milan to Rome; and there, during the first few months of the following year, I worked my way through the second typescript. I wasn't able to work every day, and the best of days were at most a question of two or three typewritten pages—of a total of five hundred. No more than two or three pages, since then I'd begin to feel faint, and it made no sense to try to push on further. In any case, I had managed to set up a rhythm, no matter how laborious, when two new facts transpired and plucked me again away from it. My Florentine publisher discontinued my modest stipend—throwing me into desperation and forcing me to pass along to another company, to the one in Milan. And at much the same time—the new contract had just been signed—the apartment directly above my own was rented to people who were anything but tranquil. The world, yes, is full of people like that—in constant need of movement and parties, and without regard for neighbors—and surely there's no point in belaboring any single case. But for me it marked disaster, and moreso for *Toledo*.

The project already had met with approval on the part of my new Milanese publisher, and just as the company's editor was starting to ask—justly, I think, since I don't have much experience with this sort of thing—that I show a bit more attention to the text (this now was the third draft) and establish firm control of form, no less than of the flow of *experience*, the anguished state of mind I had known in Via Mulino delle Armi presented itself again, and this time around I could see no hope. Or, to state things more precisely, the only hope I managed to descry, after several months of useless protest, lay in building a kind of hut in the center of my room (which luckily was a rather large room): first a compartment in which to write (at the then considerable cost of a quarter of a million Lire) and it required several months, but a place in which to write struck me as more important than a place in which to sleep; and then, the following year, a second compartment for a bedroom, which had shown itself to be utterly indispensable if I wanted really to write, and not simply to copy things out on the typewriter. It hardly needs to be added that the air in these two huts inside my room was very limited. The room had only a tiny window, covered by a screen. The whole situation had brought me to the verge, or nearly, of physical collapse, and I started to hear my publisher's injunctions—the company was keeping an eye on my work—as still more noise; a noise that made me desperate, and I found it ever harder to obey. Finally, indeed, I no longer obeyed at all.

The whole tragicomic affair found its culmination in year three: the third year of my living so absurdly in my Roman hut. My building, here again, as before in Milan, was thrown into the turmoil of renovation, for a whole pitiless year.

This was also the year of the cholera epidemic, and all these sources of anxiety—the summer heat, the danger of cholera, the bricklayers, the dust, and my work necessarily set aside—wore away at me relentlessly. The things that the publisher had to say about my work fell on an ear that by now was utterly deaf to them. Such a horrid period! And laden with all the reasons for my having started out by talking of the writer who comes from nowhere, and then returns into nowhere. I had known no education and remained incapable of any appropriation of the physical and social world; otherwise I would never have sailed my boat onto such remote shoals: the shoals of my need for self-expression.

But why talk about it? Now it's all over. No matter the way that book got written, I feel that its pages—at least the first of them—allowed me to save, or at least to attempt to illuminate, the feeling of strangeness that lies in the way the world takes shape in the eyes of a child—a girl, in this particular case—who hasn't been sufficiently apprised of its nature and structure. Its mystery then collapses on top of such children and destroys them. (Their sense of enchantment remains, but the look of the world turns grave.) It strikes me also that in the second part of the book (despite the unfortunate, irreparable cleavage dividing it from the first) I have somehow depicted the lengthy shadow or shadows of a destiny that meshes with the course of things in general (the war, the power of a few over all the creatures of the youthful world, the tardy perception of the rights denied to each of us, the subsequent lament). I haven't offered much more than that, and what little I may have offered unfortunately lapses into illegibility, not only owing to my own almost convulsive mode of self-expression, but also to the ever more virulent phenomenon to which I referred above: to the ever greater loss of the knowledge of language, as a result of the workings of the mass media: a phenomenon, by now, which has even invaded the universities. It strikes me too that this loss of the knowledge of language—at the national level—derives from an even more grave and terrible loss of the vibrant sensation of being alive. In Biblical times, and up until not too long ago, this feeling was indivisible from all cognition of the life of the earth itself. One knew the implications of an apple, a horse, the setting and rising of the sun. Such things today no longer speak to us. How could we demand that language—that always new and never-changing symbol of the whole of our sublime and terrestrial world—now reawaken those images? Like the image, for example, of love! With the figure of the young bourgeois who approaches a separate and wholly unknown world—the world of the gates of the port, of the hovels of the poor, the world of the deformed—who approaches Damasa—I meant to say that love contains nothing real (as reality is currently defined). It consists wholly of the pain and splendor of incipient knowledge. It's entirely a fact of hidden and majestic equilibriums, no different, for example, than those that accomplish the spectacle of springtime, the implosion of stars, or the way the stars appear before us, broaching incommensurable epochs. But none of that—in a culture now based on material objects (and such a culture, for the moment, is perhaps a necessity)—any longer means anything.

Fine. I feel at this point that there isn't much more to say about the species of artist I have been describing: the artist who comes from nowhere and then returns back into it, having followed an erroneous path, outside the walls of the human, or social, city—where time is another.

I finished *Toledo* in 1975. It had taken six years—between one desperation and another. It wasn't legible. As soon as it appeared, it disappeared. Authors who haven't made themselves legible don't sell, and that was the way things ended up. The sale of the book never got off the ground, and it was even withdrawn from various bookstores. Once again I had no money, or nothing more than pocket change. So I abandoned my huts in the capital and left for Liguria before the year was out. At the start I lived in a house that was flailed by every wind—winds that were often quite terrible—and which stood in the midst of a landscape that showed not a sign of human life. The various trials I had recently experienced—as well as this condition of intolerable isolation—caused me to suffer from curious nervous disturbances. Every night—for a good half hour—I seemed to hear a group of little boys—a whole school class—running in a whirlwind up and down the stairs; yet everything was quiet. I would get up in a cold sweat and wander around the immense, silent terrace. Or, on seeing a fire in the woods on the high, surrounding hills, I'd be suddenly convinced that the war had resumed, and I seemed to hear gunfire and the screams of people in flight. One night, at about three o'clock—it was autumn, and raining—I was out on the terrace and saw a lightning bug hovering in front me, with its tiny lantern; and since it had been dozens of years since I had last seen a lightning bug, and remarking as well that now it was autumn, I believed myself to be in the presence—please pardon my effusive expression—of all that remained eternal of a kindly friend (in reality I had never met him) who had died a while before, quite obscurely, in Rome. He had written words of praise—for me, for *Toledo*—which others had then been quick to reject and refute. I seemed to hear singing. On another morning, a great rosy light shone from no apparent source into a gray November sky and shed its illumination on the mountains and the sea, the farmhouses, the steeple crosses, the villas that were scattered here and there in the dull green landscape.

In short, I was no longer able to recover from a true and proper breakdown that exhausted all of my resources, and I attempted and finally managed (already it seemed an act of grace, as later, indeed, became the general rule) to find a new house. I moved into the center of town. But since this is a tourist city—only a few remaining postcards attest to what was once the peace of Liguria's Levantine coast—I was confronted all over again with the mayhem of the cities I had abandoned: the eternal flow of traffic, the dire summer heat and cacophony, the loudmouths, the cranks, the fog, the nighttime crowds, the wailing sirens, the bands that blare their music all day long on Sundays and in the spring. Not to mention the insipid holidays with their high-flying fireworks—one might as well say bombardments—which hour after hour make the houses tremble, starting in May and recurring throughout the summer, and which kill, I imagine, so many birds.

But winter is sweet and motionless; it is also poor, and therefore livable; and certainly in this city I was sure to accomplish something. But to begin with I had no money, and I had to finish revising a few older things (like *Cappello piumato*). The slumps and magical impressions (magical and fearful) that had marked my arrival into the area were also to return. I was ill, too. And finally, here again, in this dilapidated building, urban money—the new money—was to make its appearance and demand its privileges. The old tenants were sent away; everything was sold; and again I was faced with a Renovation. Which for me is the name of a true and ghastly monster.

This last year...I don't even want to talk about it. I used a stairway which nearly had ceased to exist. Dust and detritus everywhere. A worker, one day, took to kicking at my door: he had said that he couldn't do his work if it didn't stay open all morning long, and I hadn't been willing to put up with that. I not only had a run-in with the building's owners, but finally clashed with the foreman as well. I told him he couldn't keep his workers hammering for ten hours a day (rather than eight) and that otherwise I would *kill somebody*.

Yes, I spoke these words without realizing it. They told me about it later, and my surprise and contrition were enormous, since I have never thought it permissible to raise a hand against another living creature, not even a mosquito. My run-ins with mosquitoes have indeed been very rare, no more than two or three. And now to hurl such words at a workman, me!

Yet it happened. And if I laugh about it now, I don't laugh broadly. This episode led me to think through a number of things; and a great, melancholy understanding of so many ills made its way forward. If I myself—a person already fatigued, and thrown off balance, and considerably subdued by my awareness of my nothingness—could react in such a grave and reprehensible way against a workman whose lust for activity interrupted my desperate need to think, and stood in the way of my attempt—as everything for decades has stood in its way—to express myself, what then will be the fate of the generations for whom this will or destiny of self-definition never finds realization at all? The enjoyment and consuming of goods which others have produced—things through which others have expressed themselves—seems a happy lot to people who have money. But it isn't. Buying and enjoying are in no way essential; what's essential is to make and think on one's own. For the child of the slums, for the child of the great majority.

And now I have truly finished.

I'd like to be able to hope that my moral dilemmas will little by little find a resolution, and likewise those of the younger generations. So, I'd like to cry out to everyone—defying the din of hammers that sing their painful music from every point of the horizon—I'd like to cry out: let all human beings be creative, making something with their hands or their heads, at any and every age, and especially in early youth. Allow them to learn the mysterious laws of aesthetic structure and composition—all other laws can recede—if you are truly committed to freedom and a sense of community on this fast and fleeting meteor which is life itself, surrounded by all the absence of life (by all the bleak endurance) of which the rest of the Universe appears to consist. Make a place for *aesthetics*—and its laws—within this prison, this dullness, of human life. You will have made a place for freedom—the suspension of pain—for elegance, for tenderness.